Brothers Boyfriends and Babe Magnets

Brothers
Boyfriends
and
Babe
Magnets

Kathryn Lamb

Piccadilly Press • London

For Daniel, Octavia and Alexandra.

First published in Great Britain in 2006
by Piccadilly Press Ltd,
5 Castle Road, London NW1 8PR
www.piccadillypress.co.uk

A catalogue record for this book is available from
the British Library

ISBN: 1 85340 818 2 (trade paperback)
EAN: 9 781853 408182

1 3 5 7 9 10 8 6 4 2

Printed and bound in Great Britain by Bookmarque Ltd
Cover illustration by Kathryn Lamb. Cover design by Fielding Design
Text design by Textype Cambridge
Set in Soupbone, Regular Joe and Novarese

Papers used by Piccadilly Press are produced from forests grown and
managed as a renewable resource, and which conform to the
requirements of recognised forestry accreditation schemes.

Chapter 1

Natasha

'*NON!*' SOPHIE SHRIEKS, throwing herself backwards, starfish-style, onto her bed and nearly bouncing me off the edge where I am perched, trying to calm her down (as usual).

'Sophie . . .'

'NON! I said NON!' she repeats. 'Which, roughly translated, means NOOOOOO . . . I will NOT go and live in France with six chickens and a goat.'

'Come on, Sofe!' I plead with her. 'Your mum only said she *might* get a goat . . .'

'I don't care! The goat is the symbol of the star sign Capricorn – and relationships between Capricorn and Gemini – i.e. ME! – are notoriously difficult. Oh, what part of NON! don't they understand?' she howls.

Sophie is in despair because she overheard her parents discussing some mad idea they had about giving up their jobs, selling everything and moving to

I DON'T WANT TO GO TO FRANCE – JE DIS NON!

France to live off the land – Sophie's dad has always been keen on growing his own vegetables.

'French is my WORST subject!' Sophie moans. 'You don't want me to move, do you, Tash?'

'Of *course* not!' The idea of Sophie moving to another country is unthinkable – we are Best Mates Forever and I would miss her like mad – and I tell her this. 'But I don't think your parents are really serious, are they?'

'They are! I even heard Dad talking about getting a job over there teaching English. And they've been getting all these magazines about France.'

'Still – it's just an idea. Nothing's definite . . .' I am trying to reassure myself as well as Sophie. Her parents' plan is making me nervous. I don't like change. (I've had enough of it in my life, with Mum and Dad's divorce, etc.) Although changing the subject might be a good idea, judging by the way Sophie's face is quivering as if she is about to cry.

Feeble Attempt at Changing the Subject Number One:
'It's nearly Easter!' I exclaim. 'Chocorama time!' Sophie lurves chocolate, and so do I. 'The day after tomorrow we get to totally indulge our chocoholic cravings – we can forget diets and stuff our faces with lovely, lovely choccies . . .'

'And get fat and spotty,' Sophie remarks. 'The calendar says it's Good Friday today – more like Bad Friday.'

Feeble Attempt at Changing the Subject Number Two:
'OK,' I say, brightly. 'We need to lighten up. Let's talk about boys.'

Sophie bursts into tears.

'Oh, Sofe! What's wrong?' I put my arm round her shoulders.

'I still . . . I still . . . I still . . .' she sobs.

'OK, honey – take it easy. You still what?'

'I still like him,' says Sophie in a small voice.

'Who?'

'Who do you think? Luke!'

'What? After he dumped you for several hundred other girls?' Whoops! Wrong thing to say.

'I dumped HIM!' Sophie retaliates.

'Yes . . . yes . . . I know you did – sorry! And you were RIGHT to dump him. I'm GLAD I dumped Rob – at least, I think I am . . .'

'Are you? You know Luke and Jasmine broke up again and now he's going out with Lydia. Jasmine and Lydia really have it in for each other! Remember when I spat popcorn down Lydia's neck?'

'Yes . . .'

'And she's invited us to her party the week after next, JUST TO RUB IT IN!'

'What, the popcorn?'

'NO! The fact that she's going out with Luke and we're two sad idiots without boyfriends who'll be dancing round our handbags at her party – except that I won't be there because I'm not going.'

'I don't have a handbag – mine broke,' I remark.

'So. You don't have a boyfriend OR a handbag.'

'What does it matter?' I protest. I don't want to dwell on the fact that I have mixed feelings about breaking up with Rob. He definitely cared more about his bike than he did about me. But he also has a BUM-TO-DIE-FOR!!!

'Luke's going out with Lydia and Rob's going out with his bike,' I say, finally. 'That's just how it is. I thought we'd agreed that it's better being Best Mates Forever than it is having boyfriends.'

'I suppose so . . .' says Sophie, slowly. 'Except when we're at Lydia's party.'

I peer over her shoulder at the Diary/Sketchbook where she has been scribbling down her innermost thoughts and feelings. 'You can read it,' she says, pushing the sketchbook at me, open on a page where it says:

Good Things About Boyfriends:
Having one.

Bad Things About Boyfriends:
Not having one.

I sigh deeply.

Less Feeble and More Determined Attempt at Changing the Subject:
'Could you cheer up, please – just a little bit? For me?' I say, cajolingly, touching her arm. 'It's Alfie's christening next weekend – remember?'

'Of course I remember,' Sophie replies, smiling for the first time in what seems like ages. She is coming to stay with me at my dad's house for the christening, at which my big sister Kezia and I are going to be Alfie's godparents. I feel nervous and excited about this, and I am glad that Sophie is going to be with me. It is doubly exciting as this will be the first time that Sophie has come with me to stay at Dad's house. She was meant to come before but she was ill, and then Dad and Wendy went on holiday, so in the end we decided that she should come for the christening. Kezia is driving us to Dad's house in a week's time.

'I can't believe it's so soon!' I exclaim. 'I can't wait! You'll meet Alfie – and Wendy too. She's OK.' I like Wendy, but I don't want to sound too enthusiastic out of respect for Mum – it might hurt her feelings if I raved on about Dad's new

BARRY

wife, even though Mum now has a boyfriend. His name is Barry and she met him through work. He is very quiet and wears glasses, and all they ever seem to do together is watch television – it is *so* unfair that Mum has a television in her room, and I don't! 'Dad and Wendy might take us shopping in Ditchfield,' I continue. 'And I can show you the drop-dead gorgeous assistant in that clothes shop, Grip . . .'

'The one whose feet you fell at?'

'I tripped – don't remind me! But that was ages ago – I'm sure he smiled at me last time I was there! It's going to be great, Sofe – so if you could just put off microwaving your head till we get back . . .'

'Sure. Oh my God!'

'What?'

'I haven't checked my horoscope!' Sophie brandishes the latest edition of *Lurve* magazine at me. A giveaway booklet drops out of it, entitled 'How to be a Total Babe', but Sophie is only interested in her horoscope. 'Listen to this!' she exclaims. 'It says: *Your Babe of Destiny is waiting in the wings!*'

'Wings? Babe of Destiny?' I repeat, totally confused.

'It's a theatrical term!' Sophie explains. 'It means there's someone out there for me – a special someone – my Fate Mate! It's only a matter of time!'

'I could have told you that.'

'Hang on – Luke likes acting! So the theatrical term could be significant.'

'The only significant thing is how gullible you are, Sofe! Those horoscopes are rubbish. Look at mine: *Beware! Your Spring Fling could turn into your Summer Bummer!* What on earth does that mean?'

'No idea. Put some music on. My soul needs soothing.'

I flip on a CD, expecting to hear the Melodics' latest album, *Forgotten Girl*, which Sophie and I have been listening to non-stop since it was released. But instead we get *Classic Dance Trance Ibiza House Volume* 26 with the mega-blast surround sound knob turned up to maximum parental irritation level.

'Kyle!' Sophie yells out of her bedroom door. 'Now I know you *were* in my room earlier when I was at Tash's –

you left your stupid CD in my machine! Stop using *my* CD player!'

'Would someone PLEASE turn that AWFUL noise OFF!?!' shouts Sophie's mum from downstairs. 'It's making the windows rattle!'

'Sorry, Mum!'

As I remove the CD from the player, Kyle walks into Sophie's room, grinning, followed by Twizzler. Twizzler

TWIZZLER is next door's squashed-faced ginger-version of a Persian cat, whom Sophie's family is looking after while the neighbours are away on an Easter break. Twizzler has developed a strange devotion to Kyle and follows him everywhere, purring like a furry road drill – this is probably because Kyle is always feeding him scraps.

'Why *were* you in my room, anyway?' Sophie demands, snatching the CD and refusing to give it to Kyle until he answers her.

'Looking for clues,' he replies.

'Clues to what?'

'The female mind.'

'What? Oh – I know what this is about,' says Sophie. 'Your girlfriend! Jolene! The one in our Year who wears very short skirts?'

'She's not my . . . well . . . she might be . . . I mean . . . she . . . er . . .'

'She's your girlfriend?' suggests Sophie, coaxingly.
'Yes.'

'Wooooh hoooh!' Sophie and I sing-song, watching Kyle blush – he and Sophie both have a tendency to turn into tomatoes when they are embarrassed.

'Shut up!' says Kyle, slumping down on to the carpet and letting Twizzler walk on him and nuzzle against his face. I have noticed recently that Kyle has been constantly texting, and seems to be unaware of anything or anyone around him while he's doing it. NOW I know why!

'So you're not likely to want to leave Jolene and go and live in France, are you?' says Sophie.

'No thanks. Mum and Dad are mad. I'm staying here,' Kyle replies.

'So am I!' Sophie exclaims. 'I know – let's form the French Resistance. We'll resist the idea of moving to France! Will you help us, Tash?'

'Of course – although I'm not sure how I can . . .'

'By hiding us under the floorboards if necessary!'

'Oh, by the way . . .' says Kyle, reaching into his jeans pocket and pulling out a folded piece of paper, slightly scrumpled. 'This was pushed through the letterbox for you.' He hands it to Sophie, who unfolds it and reads, her eyes growing wider and her eyebrows rising higher by the nanosecond.

'What *is* it?' I ask impatiently, unable to contain my

curiosity now that her eyebrows have finally disappeared over the top of her head.

'It's . . . it's a poem!' Sophie replies.

'If you can call it that!' snorts Kyle. 'It's nearly as bad
as that poem you wrote to Luke which I found under
your bed . . .' His voice trails away as he notices the
steam beginning to billow out of his sister's ears.

'How DARE you read poems addressed to me!' she
explodes. 'And how DARE you go snooping under my
bed, reading things that don't concern you!'

'Pleeease – can I read it?' I plead, reaching out my
hand. (I have already seen the poem which Sophie
wrote to Luke a while ago – it *was* bad, especially since
the only word she could think of to rhyme with Luke
was 'puke'!) She hands me the piece of paper and I read
the poem. It is written in black ink with small capitals:

To the One I adore
For evermore.
I see you across the canteen
I wish I was a bean
On your plate.
Oh Let me be your Diet Coke!
My love for you is not a joke.
When we are in the same group
My heart goes loop the loop

'It's so sweet!' breathes Sophie. 'It's straight from the heart – written by a shy, sensitive soul who obviously yearns for me! For ME! Oh – how romantic!'

'It's tragic,' comments Kyle.

'It's . . .' Words fail me. (I am torn between an urge to laugh hysterically at the awfulness of the poem, an equal urge to hug Sophie in excitement and another conflicting urge to throttle her because of her tendency to gush. So I sit with my mouth hanging open . . .)

'It's definitely someone from school,' says Sophie. 'It must be my Babe of Destiny! Tash! My horoscope's already coming true! But who can it be? Oh – how bitter-sweet it is to be the object of a poet's hopeless longing!'

'Yes . . . hopeless,' I mutter. Sophie drives me mad when she switches into Full Drama Queen Mode. I would never make such a big deal out of it if I received a silly love poem. Which I haven't . . .

'It's obviously someone who can't write decent poetry to save his life!' scoffs Kyle.

'Shut up, Kyle!' Sophie retorts. 'I bet *you* couldn't write a decent poem if you tried. You're like all the other boys in Year Nine – obsessed with making rude noises and looking up girls' skirts. I don't know what Jolene sees in you.'

There is an awkward silence. Looking hurt, Kyle gets up to leave. He walks stiffly out of the room, followed by a still-purring Twizzler.

'That was a bit harsh, Sofe,' I whisper after Kyle has gone. 'He must really like Jolene. She's his first real girlfriend.' Last year Kyle went out briefly with a girl called Charlotte Steel – but this time it seems to be more serious. He must have redeeming features which Sophie and I don't always see because of his Revolting Slob tendencies, including a new and extreme-queasiness-inducing habit he has developed

KYLE

of squeezing his spots in front of us! I don't know why he wants to hang around us so much as we are not always that nice to him.

'I suppose I should have kept my mouth shut,' Sophie admits. 'But it's all getting too much for me – first France, then my horoscope, then I get a poem from an unknown admirer. Do you think it's Luke?'

'I . . . I don't know. I don't really think it's Luke's style. I don't think he's into poetry. I think it's just as well you decided not to send that poem you wrote to him.'

'I can't think of anyone who's into poetry,' Sophie sighs. 'Although it's probably something boys would keep quiet about, isn't it? I think it's reeeally sweet! I need to find out who it is! Perhaps it's that cute boy in the same geography group as me – Lewis. He's got lovely dark eyes and long lashes, and I've had the feeling for some time that he fancies me. Or perhaps it's . . .'

'Ed,' I suggest. Ed is the official Year Ten Nerd. He is tall and gangly with a thick thatch of dark, wavy hair and black-framed glasses which always seem to be slipping down his long nose so that he has to keep pushing them back up. He is the sort of boy whose school tie is longer than his body. He and his geeky friend Patrick spend most of their break-times having mock *Star Wars* battles with pretend lightsabers. 'Ed's in the same French group as you,' I add. 'And he's always scribbling things in that black notepad he carries around with him. Probably poems to you.'

Sophie looks as if she has just walked into a wall. I suppose it was mean of me to suggest Ed, but her gushing was beginning to get on my nerves – and no

ED – THE OFFICIAL YEAR TEN NERD

one is writing love poems to *me*!

'OK,' she says, quietly. 'I'm not leaving the house – in case I meet Ed. And I'm certainly not going to the library with Mum – he practically *lives* there!'

'He's not that bad – and it might not be him.'

'Nooooo!' moans Sophie. 'I think it *is* him,' (Yes – she is definitely in Full Drama Queen Mode, and will now leap, weeping and wailing to the WORST conclusions – me and my big mouth!) '– or it could even be his friend, Patrick! Help me, Tash! I need something to take my mind off EVERYTHING!'

'OK . . .'

Final and Desperate – but Inspired! – Attempt to Change the Subject:

'I know!' I exclaim. 'Let's redecorate! I'll help with your

room, and you can help with mine – a bedroom makeover!'

'Yes – I like that idea!' Sophie enthuses.

'And we could even give ourselves makeovers at the same time – if we're going to be staying in a lot,' I add, picking up the 'How to be a Total Babe' booklet. 'You probably don't need this advice, Sofe,' I say. 'You're a babe already, obviously – that's why you get poems written to you by anonymous admirers.' I flick through the booklet and find a list of top tips on becoming a Total Babe, which I read aloud to Sophie:

1) *Try our total body makeover and be a total babe! Start from the inside so eat plenty of fruit and veg and drink at least three litres of water a day!*

2) *Throw away those sweets and choccies! Your skin will glow with health and you can flash that Magnetic Smile!* ('Can we wait until after Easter to give up chocolate?' Sophie pleads.)

3) *Wax. Get rid of unwanted hair. Get a friend to depilate you. Hairy legs are soooooo NOT magnetic!*

4) *Walk tall! Strut your stuff! Practise your sexy bottom wiggle! Walk, swim, run, work that body! Get loads of healthy exercise to tone those muscles! You'll look good and feel great!*

'Sophie – what are you doing!' I ask. Sophie has jumped to her feet and seems to be impersonating a duck.

'I'm practising my sexy bottom wiggle!'

'Let me have a go!'

So we both practise sexy bottom wiggles until we collapse on to the floor in fits of helpless mirth.

'Thanks, Tash!' Sophie gasps, recovering her breath. 'I feel much better now – I'm so glad you're here!'

I'm glad too that I am staying the night with Sophie, my Best Mate Forever, even if she does keep gushing about her secret admirer in between bouts of worrying that it might be Ed. I try to distract her by suggesting that we concentrate on turning ourselves into Total Babes Forever with groovy rooms – and she agrees.

It is also a relief for me to have a break from Mum and Barry making googly eyes at each other – in the intervals when they are not watching television. I *am* trying to be pleased for Mum – I want her to be happy, and she seems more relaxed when Barry is around – but it is strange seeing her with a man who is not Dad . . .

We flick on the television – Sophie has one in her room. She is allowed to watch it after she has done all her homework, and at weekends and on holidays. Her parents are so cool, even if they have mad ideas about moving to France. I'm sure they won't *really* go. They can't! I *need* my Best Mate . . . . When Sophie isn't in Drama Queen Mode – there are intervals of sanity in out lives! – she is really good at calming *me* down and reminding me that my workaholic, Barry-obsessed mum and my absent dad really *do* care about me, and that she is always there for me . . .

Chapter 2

Sophie

IT HAS BEEN A LONG NIGHT. At times I felt exhilarated at being the object of a poet's hopeful longing – at these times I jumped up and down on the bed and hit Tash with a pillow out of sheer *joie de vivre*. It *might* be Luke! It might be Lewis! It might be another gorgeous boy called James! It could be anyone! Then the thought of Ed with his thick-lensed glasses and mouth like a dog's bum floated across my mind and I became depressed. Tash had to comfort me and tried to distract me with thoughts of a cheerful new colour scheme in my bedroom. After that I thought about having to move away from all my friends, especially Tash, and being made to live on a giant vegetable plot in the middle of France with six chickens and a goat – and I cried. Tash had to go to the bathroom and fetch the loo roll after we ran out of tissues.

Tash is looking tired. She is lying in bed watching *Good*

SIX CHICKENS AND A GOAT

Morning! with Hugo and Deirdre, the ever-cheerful presenters. I am sitting on the edge of the bed, feeling restless. I turn to look at Tash.

'Thanks for being there, Tash – sorry if I kept you awake last night.'

'It's OK. You were there for me when Mum started bringing Barry home and I was really worried he was going to move in.'

'So there's no sign of him moving in?' I ask.

'Not so far. He usually leaves late at night. But I still need to get used to the situation. He was there the other night and I realised I'd left my pants on the floor in the bathroom after I'd had a bath, but only remembered after he'd gone in there and it was too late to rush in and pick them up . . .'

'Oh my God!' I exclaim. 'How embarrassing! I would have died!'

'I died.'

'But you know you can always come here, don't you?' I tell her. 'You're *always* welcome!'

'Thanks, Sofe,' Tash says.

I give her arm an affectionate squeeze. Then I start fidgeting. 'How long is Kyle going to be in the bathroom?' I ask in exasperation. 'I need to get in there – what on earth is he doing?'

'Probably reading your magazines again – trying to find out how to make himself more attractive to Jolene! He could start by changing his socks more than once a fortnight . . .'

'You're right!' I say, picking up the booklet on How to be a Total Babe. 'This could be our opportunity to transform Kyle into a Babe Magnet! Let's create Kyle with Style! I'm fed up of living with a smelly-sock little brother – I want a Super Cool Sibling who all the girls will drool over! And he'll *surely* want to go along with our plan so that he can impress Jolene – and we'll reap the benefits too! No more in-your-face spot squeezing!'

'That's got to be worth it!' Tash agrees.

'Definitely!' I say, feeling more light-hearted now that I have not one, but three projects in mind: a new look for my bedroom, a Total Babe makeover for myself so that I look my best for the one who adores me from a distance – oh! let it be Luke or Lewis and *not* Ed – and, last and probably least, a new look for my brother.

'It's going to take some doing,' I remark, 'but Kyle is going to be incredibly cool.'

'MUM!' Kyle shouts from the bathroom. 'MUUUM!!! THERE'S NO LOO ROLL! Sophie used it all up, crying all night! I think she's got Girl Problems!'

'Oh – great!' I mutter, rolling my eyes. 'Thanks, Kyle . . .'

Mum comes running up the stairs with a loo roll for Kyle, after which she pokes an anxious face around my door. 'Is this true, Sophie, darling?' she asks in a concerned voice. 'Were you crying all night? Your eyes look a bit red – what are these Girl Problems?'

'I have no idea, Mum,' I reply, suddenly feeling that all the magic would go out of having a secret admirer if I told Mum and Dad about it. 'I think they exist only in Kyle's fevered imagination. But I really don't want to go to France!'

'Oh, Sophie!' Mum comes over and sits on the bed beside me, and gives me a big hug. 'Dad and I would never do anything that you and Kyle were unhappy about – we would only move to France if it looked like being the best possible step for the whole family.'

'But it isn't – and it never would be! Why don't you get a goat and keep it here in the back garden? Dad can go on growing vegetables – I just don't see *why* we need to move to France.' (How can I leave the one who adores me from afar? France would be tooooo far . . .)

'I'm sure you're right, darling,' says Mum, giving me another hug. 'Dad and I are just looking into possibilities, that's all. And I promise we won't do anything without consulting you and Kyle first.'

I nod, feeling slightly reassured.

'And are you sure there's nothing else bothering you?' she asks. Mum and I share a sixth sense which tells us when the people we are close to are upset about something. I hesitate, wondering whether to show her the poem. I could sacrifice some of the magic in return for some parental understanding and reassurance – except that they would probably go over the top and keep asking questions, and it would get annoying – Dad would criticise the poem for bad grammar or something . . .

'No – there's nothing else. I'm fine. Thanks, Mum.' I also ask if Tash and I can redecorate my room over the rest of the Easter break – and I explain about our plan to paint Tash's room as well. Mum thinks this is a great idea, as long as we are careful to cover all the furniture and carpets before we start painting. She offers to drive us to a big DIY store called Do-It-Together later in the morning to get paint, etc.

'Do-It-Together's open all over Easter,' she says enthusiastically. 'So there'll be no problem getting more paint if you run out. You'd better think about what colours you want – if your mum's willing, Tash, we could get the paint for your room as well. But you'd better ask her first.'

After Mum has gone, I look around my room. It has been purple for as long as I can remember, and I will miss the stencilled silver stars and signs of the zodiac if they end up being painted over. But it is definitely time for a room makeover, and I don't like to do things half-heartedly . . .

'How about orange?' I suggest.

'Orange?' Tash screws up her eyes as if someone is shining an orange light straight into them.

'Yes – orange! The colour of the future.'

'Hang on, Sofe – imagine waking up on a Monday morning – you've got a headache, your period's started, you haven't done your maths homework, there's an enormous red spot on the end of your nose, and your room is . . . orange.'

'Hmm . . . I suppose you're right. Orange is very in-your-face.'

Tash looks thoughtful. Then her face brightens. 'I've just had a brilliant idea!' she exclaims. 'Why don't we paint our rooms completely white and fill them with hundreds of lava lamps? The reflections of the coloured lights on the walls would be sooo amazing!'

'Cool!' I agree. 'But it would really only look good at night, unless we kept our curtains drawn all day. And I'm not sure if there'd be room for all our stuff AND hundreds of lava lamps.'

'You've got a point,' says Tash. 'And Mum would probably say no.'

Eventually we decide that we will both choose the best shade of blue we can find at Do-It-Together and have matching blue bedrooms.

'It will make me think of summer skies,' I say. 'Blue is meant to be restful and calming. I need that.'

'Anything will be better than the pukey green I've got on my walls at the moment,' Tash remarks. 'Mum greened the whole house after Dad left – I think it reflected the way she was feeling at the time.'

Any further discussion on the subject of Bedroom Improvement is interrupted by the arrival of Kyle, holding a folded square of lined paper . . .

Oh! Be still my beating heart!

'Found this on the doormat – I was on my way out,' he says. 'Thought I'd better bring it up to you before Mum or Dad found it. Here you are . . .' he hesitates, noticing the half-fascinated, half-alarmed expression on my face. 'Listen, sis,' he says. 'Don't let this get to you – it's just someone fooling around . . . or . . . or . . . they fancy you and they're too shy to say it to your face. I felt *really* shy and awkward before I summoned up the courage to talk to Jolene. But I'm glad I did. This boy, whoever he is . . . if he's serious . . . and if it's meant to be – it'll all work out, you'll see.'

'Er – thanks, Kyle!' I am slightly stunned by this sudden, almost poetic burst of empathy and understanding. Kyle's feminine side tends to make these occasional unexpected appearances – then he turns back into a normal brother. But I am too distracted by the piece of paper in my hands to discuss feelings with him at the moment. With trembling fingers I spread out the crumpled sheet on my lap. This time it looks as though it has been torn roughly out of a school exercise book. Written in the same small, neat black capitals, the message reads:

JE T'AIME, JE T'AIME, JE T'AIME.
I HOPE YOU FEEL THE SAME.

'Short and sweet,' Kyle remarks, peering down at the piece of paper. I think his Sensitive Moment may have come to an end. He has turned his attention to a message which he has received on his mobile, a faraway look on his face . . .

But I only have eyes for my latest love poem. Placing my fingertips on the small black letters, I say: 'This was written by my one true soul mate – I can feel his aura! So it can't be Ed . . .'

'Oh – puhleease!' Tash exclaims, rolling her eyes skywards. 'Hasn't your all-seeing third eye got us into enough trouble in the past, Sofe?'

'But it's sooo romantic!' I insist. 'He's taken the trouble to write to me in French – the language of love!'

'I thought you hated French,' Tash remarks. 'And anything to do with France.'

'This is different,' I retort. Anyone would think she was jealous . . . perhaps I have been going on about my secret admirer too much, but I can't help it – I'm so excited!

'It's definitely someone from the same French group as you, Sofe,' says Kyle, tearing his gaze away from his mobile. 'Because he's completely hopeless at French.'

'Thanks, Kyle.'

'It's only half in French and it doesn't even rhyme,' he continues, snatching the precious piece of paper from my lap and staring at it. 'And look – you can just see a squiggle of red ink along the edge of the paper, where it's been torn out of a book. Isn't that where a teacher has written a comment?'

'Oh – you're right!' I exclaim. 'That's Monsieur Dupont's writing – he always uses a red pen. So it *must* be someone from my French group! Oh – Lewis isn't in my French group . . .' I struggle to hide my disappointment.

'Ed is,' Tash remarks.

I fail to hide my dismay.

'Whoever wrote this stuff to you has a leaky pen,' says Kyle. 'There are a few smudges and splodges of ink – look.'

'You're not bad at finding clues, little brother,' I say. 'And since you're obviously fond of sleuthing – you're always snooping round my room! – do you fancy finding out who wrote this? I love having a secret admirer, but having an admirer who isn't secret might be even nicer – someone to adore me face to face. I definitely want to know who it is *before* we go back to

school next term. In fact I wouldn't mind knowing who it is in time for Lydia's party. If it's someone nice, I could go to the party with them – and they might have a friend who you could go with, Tash,' I add, generously.

'Leave it to Inspector Kyle!' my brother says, grinning. He obviously fancies himself as an undercover detective! But it is kind of

INSPECTOR KYLE

him to agree to help me. Perhaps his kindness is one of the qualities which appeals to Jolene – it certainly can't be any of his grosser habits, such as pulling up the bottom of his T-shirt and using it as a handkerchief – mega mega BLEEEE!!! 'I'll need a list of all the boys in your French group,' he adds.

'There are only seven of them – there's Luke, and Rob, and James – he's cool . . .'

'He's very cool,' agrees Tash, quickly. I know she fancies James, because I caught her staring at him and drooling – but I don't think she realises that I fancy him even more – it's just that I've been too busy fancying Luke and having my heart broken into a zillion pieces, etc. Until now.

'There's Jack and Harry – they're both cool,' I continue. 'And Will – he's cool, too . . . And Ed – he's not cool.'

'OK – no problem,' says Inspector Kyle, making notes with a stubby pencil on a scrap of paper – I manage to stop him just in time from scrawling on my precious poem, which I shall keep close to my heart forever!

'But can you find out who it is without telling anyone what this is all about?' I ask. 'I'll kill you if I get back to school and find that everyone's laughing at me! Because I *suppose* it's *possible* that someone's having a joke at my expense.' This is an awful thought, but I can be a realist, despite what Tash thinks! 'And on the other hand,' I continue, brightening, 'if it really is my Babe of Destiny, I don't want to put him off.'

'Don't worry,' says Kyle. 'I won't tell anyone what's going on. I'll use my most undercover methods – they'll cost you extra, of course.'

'Ha ha! You can forget payment – I don't have any money. But there's *something* Tash and I can do for you . . .' I explain to Kyle about our plan to turn him into a Babe Magnet.

He looks doubtful. 'I'm struggling not to take offence,' he comments. 'Surely I'm not *that* uncool that I need *help*?'

Tash and I exchange looks. Kyle mutters 'Uh oh' and makes a dash for the door, but Twizzler, who is just coming into the room, trips him up, and he lands on the carpet. I leap across the room and sit on him. 'Just listen!' I exclaim. 'We can tell you how to make Jolene fall even more in lurve with you! We're girls – we know how! It'll also save you the trouble of having to read my magazines and nose through my things – and it'll save me from having to throttle you for doing that!'

'Fine – whatever,' he gasps, struggling to break free. His mobile bleeps . . . 'I've got to go!' he says, and bolts out of the room. Tash and I exchange looks, and stifle giggles.

'We *will* turn my little brother into the Embodiment of Cool!' I say, emphatically.

* * *

Shortly afterwards Mum is ready to drive us to Do-It-Together, so Tash goes round to her mum's house to ask if she can redecorate her room and help me to do mine. Her mum says yes and gives Tash money for the paint – Tash tells me that she was in the middle of watching a film with Barry, and would probably have agreed to anything to get Tash out of the way . . .

We spend a happy half-hour at Do-It-Together, browsing amongst the paint pots, although I can't help looking over my shoulder from time to time in case anyone is watching me – I am half-expecting my secret admirer to leap out from behind the shelves and throw himself at my feet, declaring his undying love. When this doesn't happen, I feel strangely disappointed. I tell Tash.

'I think you've got to keep this in proportion,' she says, sounding irritated. 'It's just someone in your French group fooling around.'

'I know, I know . . .' Feeling silly, I turn my attention back to the paint. I wish Tash would be more encouraging – I suppose she's feeling left out because no one's worshipping her from afar.

We choose a beautiful shade of blue called Skydance, and fill our trolley with paint pots, furry rollers, trays, brushes, masking tape and white paint for the skirting-boards. We also find some rolls of a cool border design of silver stars and swirls, and Mum pays.

On the way home I think of all the work that needs to be done before the fun can start: moving furniture, taking down posters, removing the curtains, covering up the carpets, cleaning the walls.

'Hey, Tash!' I say. 'If we start with my room, can I come and stay with you? Because it's going to be such an upheaval. Can I stay at Tash's, Mum?'

'If her mum says you can,' Mum replies.

'But I want to start painting my room,' says Tash. 'I can't wait to see what it looks like! So my room's going to be an upheaval, too. Wait a minute – I know what we can do! We'll move in with Kezia for the weekend! She's got a huge room – so one of us can share her double bed and the other can sleep on her sofa bed!'

'But won't she mind? What about Geoffrey?' Geoffrey is Kezia's carrot-haired boyfriend.

'Geoffrey's gone to stay with his family for Easter – so there's no problem!' Tash exclaims.

No problem. I have a feeling that the phrase 'No problem' qualifies as Famous Last Words . . .

'WHAT?' shrieks Kezia, hands on hips. 'No WAY are you two idiots bunking up in MY room!'

'Oh, pleeease, Kez! It'll be FUN!' Tash pleads. 'When did you last have a proper sleepover? A real girls' night in?'

'A complete idiots' night in, you mean,' retorts Kezia.

'I can give you a relaxing shoulder massage,' I offer.

'I can think of better ways to relax,' Kezia snaps, ungratefully. 'Such as by NOT being here! You can have my room IF you guarantee, under pain of death, NOT to touch ANY of my things. I'll go and stay with my mate Fran – at least she's sane!'

Kezia texts Fran to ask her if she can come to stay, but Fran texts back to say that she can only have Kezia for one night – tomorrow.

'Looks like you're stuck with us!' says Tash. I don't think the note of triumph in her voice is helping matters . . .

'I know!' I exclaim, thinking of a way to cheer Kezia up and stop her changing her mind about sharing her room. 'Let's get Easter off to a flying start – let's have a Midnight Feast of Chocolate!'

YUM!

CHOCCY DUCKIES

MAJOR CHOCFEST!

Kezia, who is a serious chocoholic, is finally persuaded and she produces several large chocolate eggs and assorted bags and tubes of mini-eggs which she has been hiding away in her room. There is also a giant chocolate chicken which Geoffrey left for her. Tash adds a box of chocolates which she bought for us to share, and I fetch the chocolate bunnies which I bought for everyone. We lay it all out in front of us.

I feel that I have died and gone to chocoholic heaven . . .

Chapter 3

Natasha

I FEEL THAT I HAVE DIED. And I am also getting a cold.

'I feel sick!' groans Sophie.

I am inclined to think that the Midnight Feast of Chocolate was a mistake. I never want to see another chocolate as long as I live.

Sophie and I are both squashed on to the sofa bed, since Kezia insisted on her right to hog the whole of the double bed and is currently spread out on it in her underwear, having thrown off the duvet when she got too hot. This is not a sight that helps with the queasy feeling.

'She is sooo selfish!' I hiss at Sophie.

'I heard that!' snarls Kezia. 'This is *my* room – remember?'

It is a shame that we seem to be starting Easter Day with a joint grumping session. Kezia was a lot of fun to be with last night, joking and laughing and helping us with our plan to turn Kyle into a Babe Magnet. She was even kind and understanding – this has been known to happen from time to time; she has been sweet and supportive and big sisterly towards me on a number of occasions when I have found myself falling apart. Last night she gave plenty of wise advice to Sophie on the subject of anonymous poets and how she shouldn't get her hopes up of getting back together with Luke as he has already hurt her once and would probably do so again . . .

But this morning Kezia is a mega-grump.

'Can't you two shut up?!' she yells at us. 'You kept me awake all last night with your silly giggling!'

'Hah!' I shout derisively. (I do a good derisive 'Hah!') 'What about you, snoring all night! I didn't get a wink of sleep – it sounded like there was a ten-ton truck rolling backwards and forwards across the room!'

'Er – would anyone like a relaxing shoulder massage?' Sophie offers, tentatively. 'Or I could go and make everyone a nice cup of tea?'

'I do NOT snore!' yells Kezia, ignoring her.

'You DO!' I yell back. 'You're like a walrus on heat!'

'For God's sake keep it down in there!' yells Mum from the room next door. 'Some of us are trying to sleep! Oh – Happy Easter, by the way! I think the Easter Bunny's been – he's left eggs for you all downstairs!'

Sophie groans.

'Happy Easter, Mum!' I call out.

'Um – I think I'd better go and wish my own family a happy Easter,' says Sophie. 'And I need some fresh air.'

'Good idea – can I come with you?' I ask. 'I need a break from this madhouse . . .'

Kezia is ignoring us and already packing her overnight bag to go and stay with Fran.

It is a beautiful sunny morning. I wish I felt better – my throat is sore and I keep thinking I am going to sneeze – and then I don't. And I feel sick after all that chocolate. Sophie and I need to do some serious rethinking about the Total Babe Effect Strategy – we have strayed some-what. I think I will suggest drinking pure water to cleanse our bodies, thinking pure thoughts to cleanse our minds, and giving each other a facial. But as we open the gate to walk up Sophie's garden path, something rustles in the bushes. Sophie gives an excited shriek.

'Aargh! It's him! The poet!' she shouts, clutching my arm.

'No – you idiot!' I reply. 'It's Twizzler.' Sophie is driving me mad with her obsession with anonymous poets and secret admirers! If I had a secret admirer – which I haven't because life is unfair – I wouldn't go on and on about it . . .

A dishevelled Twizzler emerges from the bushes, leaves and twigs stuck to his thick ginger coat. 'We ought to groom him,' I suggest. 'I know – let's ask

Granny if we can borrow that brush she uses to groom Crumpet.' (Granny is not my real Granny but a sweet elderly lady whom we once helped around the house while her daughter was away. Crumpet is her dog, whom we take for walks on Sunday – Easter Sunday is no exception.)

'Wha . . . what's that?' asks Sophie quietly, her voice quivering.

'I told you – it's Twizzler. Don't be fooled by his cunning disguise of leaves and twigs.'

'No – I mean – on the doorstep!' She points with a trembling finger.

'Oh my God!' I exclaim. On the doorstep is the most enormous box of chocolates I have ever seen, with a heart-shaped balloon attached to it.

Sophie approaches the box of chocolates gingerly, as if it is about to explode. 'There's a note with it!' she whispers to me.

'Well – read it!' I whisper back.

'It says: *You don't really need these – you're sweet enough already.*'

'Wow!' I whisper, sighing inwardly – Sophie is going to be even more of a Drama Queen now! 'Someone knows you like chocolate. Can we stop whispering now?' I say, trying to sound casual and like I don't care.

'Yes,' whispers Sophie, barely able to speak with excitement.

Upstairs in her room, surrounded by stuff piled on to her bed which has been pushed into the middle of the floor prior to painting, Sophie has regained her voice.

'I suppose I really AM a Total Babe,' she sighs, brushing her pale blond hair back from her clear-skinned face with its light sprinkling of freckles, and gazing at me out of summer-sky eyes. 'The boys can't resist me . . .'

Oh no – she's going to start gushing again!

'Only *one* boy . . .' I point out.

'As far as we know,' says Sophie dreamily, unwrapping one of *those* chocolates and popping it into her mouth. (I guess that Sophie can handle eating chocolate again as they are from her admirer, making them doubly delicious!)

'You won't be a Total Babe if you keep eating chocolate

like that!' I snap. 'You'll be a Walking Zit! Have you forgotten our plan to transform ourselves? Or don't you care?'

I feel annoyed. No one has given *me* chocolates – or a balloon. And my cold feels worse. I glance down at my phone. I haven't had a message for ages, apart from the usual one from Mum – WHERE ARE YOU? – which she seems to send at random intervals throughout the day. Rob isn't exactly falling over himself to get back together with me – I don't know how I'd feel if Sophie and Luke got back together but Rob wasn't interested in *me*. Would I be concerned about Sophie, like a Best Mate should, or would I be consumed by pathetic jealousy and a deep and guilty wish that Sophie would break out in spots all over her face and have a bad hair week or even month? I think I am turning into a Horrid Person, which is very far removed from being a Total Babe or a Best Mate.

To make matters worse, on top of having a cold I can feel a huge pimple throbbing on the end of my nose – it is about to erupt and scream, 'Look at me!'

I grab a handful of chocolates. The feeling of never wanting to see another one as long as I live has worn off . . . Chocolate is now my only source of comfort in an indifferent world.

'You're right!' exclaims Sophie, knocking the chocolates out of my hand. 'Sorry, Tash! We've got to lay off the chocolate and get stuck into the beauty treatments!

I MUST look my best for my secret admirer! Oh, Tash – it might be James! He is sooo cute, don't you think?'

'I can't say I've noticed,' I reply, untruth-fully – I spent many happy moments last term, noticing James . . .

'Don't lie!' says Sophie. 'I know you fancy him! But I promise not to rub it in your face if it turns out it's me he wants.'

JAMES

'Oh – er – thanks. I think.'

'Come on, Tash – don't be miserable! It's a lovely day for a spring fling, and I am the wind beneath a poet's wings!'

'What? Have you forgotten it might be Ed? The same Ed who looked like he was undergoing shock treatment when he danced at the school disco? The Ed with the flobbery lips which resemble a dog's bottom when he sucks them in? Imagine those lips kissing you . . .'

'Tash! Stop it! What is your problem? Best Mates are supposed to make each other feel better, not worse. Now you've got me all worried, and I *was* feeling happy! Are you jealous or something?'

'Er . . .'

'Oh, Tash – you *are* jealous! You don't need to be – you can be a Total Babe, too!'

'How? My nose looks as though it has a second, much smaller nose attached to the end of it. And having a cold is making it worse – it won't stop throbbing!'

'Hmm – that's a nasty spot,' Sophie admits. 'The chocolate can't have helped. Keep swigging from your water bottle and I'll go and boil the kettle.'

'Why?' I ask, feeling slightly alarmed – this has a lot to do with the manic glint in Sophie's eyes.

'I'm going to steam open your pores! You just pour boiling water into a bowl, chuck a tea towel over your head, and lean over it. The impurities just drop out of your face! It's like steaming vegetables! Or fish! And it'll help with your cold, too. Mum recommends a few drops of eucalyptus oil, added to the water.'

'Er, thanks, Sofe, but no thanks! I don't feel comfortable about being steamed like a fish in someone else's house. I *might* let you give me the steam treatment when we're alone in Kezia's room tonight!'

'OK – you're on!' Sophie exclaims. 'We'll make it a Total Babes' Night In!' She picks up the Total Babe booklet from amongst the piles of stuff on her bed, and flicks through it. 'Here's something else we can do!' she says, and passes the booklet to me.

Top Tip for Tip Top Tresses!

Don't forget to condition your hair so it gleams! Have a really good cut as split ends are sooooo NOT the Total Babe Look! Enhance your magnetism with a cool new hairstyle, but make sure it's not too outrageous — you don't want to put the boys off!'

'Thank you,' I say. 'But you are NOT cutting my hair! No way! I'll just be a Total Babe with a huge spot on the end of my nose and a streaming cold!' But I realise that Sophie is trying to cheer me up like a Best Mate should — and she has stopped warbling on about her admirer, which is a relief . . .

'No, no! Of course I wouldn't dream of cutting your hair! We'll get *that* done professionally. But I've got an idea for a style that would really suit you — and it doesn't involve any cutting!' Sophie enthuses. 'I'm sure I've got some bands, and where's my hairbrush? Oh — I left it at your house . . . Never mind — I can just scoop your hair with my hands.'

Shortly afterwards I look down into a mirror which is lying on the floor — not a good angle from which to view your reflection — and see that Sophie has given me two funky handlebar bunches. I look like Crumpet the dog.

Sophie is scribbling something in her Diary/Sketchbook — probably a drawing of me looking as unlike a Total Babe as it is possible to look. 'I think I'd rather concentrate on turning Kyle into a Babe Magnet,' I comment. 'Let's give him the steam treatment!'

'Oh — I forgot about Kyle!' exclaims Sophie. 'We ought to tell him about the chocolates! It's crucia evidence for the investigation – another vital clue that will eventually lead to the unmasking of my admirer!'

Clutching the nearly empty chocolate box in one hand and her sketchbook in the other, Sophie heads for Kyle's room. Her parents must be enjoying the sunshine in the garden – they don't seem to be in the house. Inspector Kyle is still asleep, sprawled on his bed in a very

FUNKY HANDLEBAR BUNCHES

old T-shirt with holes in it, and his boxers. We have to pick our way through the mess and debris that make up his bedroom.

'This place is a pigsty!' Sophie exclaims, waking Kyle up.

'It's a tip,' I agree.

'Mind those socks!' warns Sophie. 'They're a health hazard. Did you know that they use Kyle's socks in biological warfare? An entire continent was wiped out recently by just one pair.'

I give a low whistle.

'What's this?' mumbles Kyle, sleepily. 'A "How

KYLE'S SOCKS (ASSORTED)

CAKED IN MUD 'STAND-UP-ON-THEIR-OWN' VARIETY

'VINTAGE' VARIETY

FASCINATING TO THE CAT VARIETY

TOO MUCH EVEN FOR THE CAT VARIETY

Disgusting is Your Brother's Bedroom" reality TV show?'

'Yup. And we came to show you this.' Sophie hands Kyle the chocolate box. 'It was on the doorstep when we got here. You can read the note.'

'What? You mean someone left you an empty box of chocolates?'

'No – it was full.'

'I don't believe it! You mean to say – you *ate* the

evidence?! I suppose I should be grateful you left the box. Weren't you listening when Mum used to tell us never to accept sweets from strangers?'

'We kept a few for you,' I say, indicating a handful of chocolates at the bottom – the ones which Sophie wouldn't let me eat! 'Happy Easter!'

Kyle looks up at me blearily. 'Hi, Tash!' he says. 'Why have you turned into a dog? And no one told me it was Red Nose Day . . .'

Sophie catches up with me in the bathroom where I am tearing out the bands from my handlebar bunches and struggling to regain my composure, and *not* break down and cry because my life is so awful and I look like a freak – and I really don't want my nose to go even redder than it already is!

'For goodness sake, Tash!' Sophie pleads with me, her arm round my shoulders. 'Take no notice of him – he was just being Kyle. It was pretty average brother behaviour.'

'Then I'm glad I don't live with a brother like Kyle,' I say, moodily.

'He *did* notice, just now, that he'd upset you – if that's any consolation,' she adds, 'because I gave him one of my looks! He was saying sorry just as you were running out of the room!'

'I didn't hear,' I said. But I feel a bit better – I suppose Kyle isn't *that* bad. I remember how he was very kind to us after we split up with Rob and Luke. He also hates it if Sophie and I fall out, and does everything he can to get us back together . . .

'To be honest,' Sophie continues, 'there have been times when I've wished I didn't have a brother! But then Kyle has one of his sensitive moments and I change my mind. So I've made this list – have a look!' She hands me her sketchbook, open on a double-page spread with a heading on either side:

<u>Good Things About Brothers</u>
1) You can borrow their CDs, if their taste in music isn't too awful. Ditto books/DVDs, etc.

2) They have gorgeous friends.

3) They take the heat off you because they're always doing daft things.

<u>Bad Things About Brothers</u>
1) They borrow your stuff without asking and then lose it.

2) They have smelly friends.

3) They get away with stuff which you don't.

4) They mainly stay out of your way unless they are of the small and annoying variety.

5) They are sometimes Kind, will stick up for you, etc.

4) They hog the TV, PlayStation, etc.

5) They tease you and make you blush.

6) Their rooms smell.

7) Their socks smell.

8) They make rude noises and laugh over-loudly at their own stupid jokes.

9) They eat the entire contents of the fridge.

10) They put live frogs in your school shoes.

'Er, Sophie,' I say, hesitantly. 'There seem to be a lot more bad things about brothers than good things.'

'Exactly. Which is precisely why we made this plan.' She turns to the back of her sketchbook, where she has slipped in the piece of paper on which we wrote down our ideas for making Kyle cool. The plan reads as follows:

From Beastly Brother to Babe Magnet in Five Easy Steps:

1) He should have sexy messed-up hair, which should be clean and not full of dandruff, small living organisms, chewing-gum, leaves, twigs, etc. He should avoid flat hair and hat hair and the Curse of the Side Parting.

2) He must not sniff, spit, swear, pick his nose, scratch his bum, dig out his own - or anyone else's - earwax, fart, burp, or in any other way bore, embarrass or totally gross out his girlfriend.

3) He should try thinking about how his girlfriend might be feeling. He should say things like: 'And how are you?' It is important to get the accent on the right word. This is very challenging to the average brother. He should let his girlfriend

choose which film they go to see. This is also very challenging since he would much rather see 'Revenge of the Mutant Zombie Mice' than 'My Sweetest Love' starring Brad Chesthair and Lavinia Drip.

4) He should hold doors open for his girl-friend, preferably doors that she wants to go through (not just random doors). He should give her flowers and chocolates and write her love poems.

5) He must change his socks frequently and leave his trainers outside the door after removing them at the end of a long hot day.

'I think it's a lot to remember,' I comment. 'And you're right about it being challenging. Subtlety isn't Kyle's strongest point.'

Cue Kyle hammering on the bathroom door, demanding to know how long we're going to be as he wants a crap. Sophie opens the door and drags him into the bathroom, running her hand through his hair. 'There!' she exclaims. 'Your hair's not too bad! We just need to sort out the rest of you!'

'You're mad!' he exclaims. 'Just let me use the bath-room before I . . .'

'Ssh!' hisses Sophie. 'Just mind what you say!'

Kyle rolls his eyes, then turns to me briefly. 'Sorry if I was rude to you just now, Tash – I didn't mean to upset you.'

'That's OK,' I reply, graciously. (Kyle *can* be nice!)

Cut to twenty minutes later and Kyle is ready to go out. He's meeting up with Jolene. Sophie and I pounced on him when he came out of the bathroom and made him go back in and wash his face and brush his teeth. Then we borrowed some of Sophie's dad's expensive after-shave so that Kyle now smells amazing. We made him change his T-shirt and promise never EVER to use it as a handkerchief again! Then we gave him full instructions on how he should behave and gave him a single red rose from the bunch in the vase downstairs to give to Jolene.

'I feel stupid,' says Kyle. 'Why would she want a flower?'

Sophie and I groan in unison. 'She's a *girl*, Kyle – girls always want flowers!'

'Talking of flowers,' says Sophie, 'my secret admirer has sent me poems and chocolates – but isn't it about time he sent me flowers?'

I sigh deeply. 'You don't want much, do you?' I say, sarcastically.

After Kyle has gone we decide to get down to some serious painting as Sophie is keen to see what her

KYLE WITH STYLE

room is going to look like when it turns blue. We agree to carry on painting my room when we go back to my house this evening for our Total Babes' Night In. (I am very glad that we are staying in as my cold is making me feel like not doing much.)

Sophie's mum and dad come to wish us a happy Easter and to admire the great splash of Skydance Blue which now covers one wall. Sophie's mum gives us a chocolate rabbit each and urges us to join her in the garden soon as it is such a lovely day outside.

'We could eat lunch in the conservatory,' she says. 'It might even be warm enough to have the doors open. It's certainly the warmest Easter Day I can remember!'

It is still a beautiful day when we go to visit Granny after lunch. Crumpet is overjoyed to see us and goes

completely mad, career-
ing around the garden at
high speed, barking loudly.

CRUMPET

We take him for a walk.
Sophie keeps looking over
her shoulder to see if someone
is following us.

'I don't want it to be Ed,'
she says. 'But I wouldn't
mind if one of the other
boys rushed up to me with
a huge bunch of flowers – or
just one flower.'

I wouldn't mind if something like that happened to
me – life is so unfair!

I cheer up when we are back at Granny's house
though, drinking tea and eating biscuits. Granny gives
us a little bag of chocolate eggs each. I feel bad because
we have not brought anything for Granny, apart from my
cold germs, but she assures us that she already has far
more chocolate than she can possibly eat on her own.

Sophie tells her about the poems and the chocolates, and Granny says she is glad to hear that there is
still some romance in the world.

'So you think it's OK to have a secret admirer?'
Sophie asks.

'Yes – as long as the young man in question is some-

GRANNY

one from your class,' Granny replies. 'I'd be worried if it was someone you didn't really know. But it all sounds quite harmless to me. I expect he is very shy and is worried that you might reject him – poets are such sensitive souls! I knew a poet once – his name was Wilfred and he wrote a poem especially for me. He said that my hair was like spun gold, and he wanted us to be together as we grew old. He was killed in the war.'

'Oh! That's so sad!'

'Not really, dear. You see, I kept the poem that he wrote for me – I've kept it all these years. So part of him is still with me, even now.' Granny smiles a gentle, faraway smile, and her face softens and looks incredibly beautiful.

Sophie mentions her parents' idea of moving to France, and the expression on Granny's face changes abruptly.

'You don't want to have anything to do with the French, dear,' she says, through very thin lips. 'I knew a Frenchman once.' And she refuses to say any more on the subject – her lips are now sealed. Instead she starts talking about the weather, before asking after our families. She says that we can borrow Crumpet's dog-brush to groom Twizzler as long as we bring it back in the next few days and clean it thoroughly . . .

Back at my house (otherwise known as the Madhouse) . . .

'I wonder what the Frenchman did to Granny?' I muse, wielding a roller covered in Skydance Blue. One of my walls is nearly done already – it looks good. No more post-divorce green!

'I can't imagine,' says Sophie. 'In fact I don't *want* to imagine. But it's given me an idea of how to put Mum and Dad right off the idea of ever moving to France . . .'

But before Sophie can explain her idea, I am called to the phone to speak to Dad. He wishes me a happy Easter and says how much he is looking forward to seeing me next weekend for the christening.

Hearing his voice suddenly brings the reality of the christening much closer, and I feel happy and excited. Dad says that I sound as if I have a cold, and he hopes that I will be better in time for the christening. It's nice to get some sympathy at last – it seems to be in short supply round here! I can't talk to him for long as Kezia is waiting impatiently beside me – she wants to speak to him again – and Dad promises to send me a message on my mobile.

'Send me LOTS of messages, Dad!' I tell him. 'I haven't had any texts for AGES – no one loves me!'

Dad laughs. 'I love you loads!' he says.

'Love you too – bye!' I say.

Kezia takes the receiver and glares at me – I have left smudges of blue paint all over it. But I don't care – I feel happy! I would have liked to have asked Dad what he thinks about Mum having a boyfriend called Barry, and whether he thinks it is normal for me to feel jealous and occasionally wish that Barry would be blasted into space on a special mission which would involve him not returning to Earth for at least ten years . . . But it would have been difficult to talk with Mum and Barry sitting there in the room – so I will save it for next weekend.

About five minutes later my phone goes blip blip bleeeep! I read the message from Dad: CAN'T WAIT TO SEE YOU! DON'T GROW UP TOO FAST. DAD.

I smile and hug my phone. Blowing my runny nose – which makes my spot hurt – I think my chances of growing up too fast are strictly limited. But you never know! Right now I feel content with my low-excitement life. The prospect of next weekend's christening and seeing Dad again is enough . . .

I carry on painting with renewed enthusiasm, and I drink nearly two whole litres of water to celebrate. I even agree to let Sophie steam open my pores! She is bored with painting (she didn't get so quickly bored when we were painting *her* room!) and wants to get on with the Total Babes' Night In! She also wants to take advantage of the fact that Kez has now gone to Fran's house and we have her room to ourselves!

<u>Total Babes' Night In</u>
<u>A Truthful Account by Tash</u>

1) We go downstairs to the kitchen and boil the kettle. Sophie throws a smelly old tea towel over my head and I tear it off and throw it back at her. After a lot of giggling Mum comes into the kitchen, gives us a clean tea towel and supervises the steaming of my pores and blocked nose. This is annoying – I don't need Mum's help! It is also hot and difficult to breathe – it doesn't unblock my nose but makes it a lot redder. I emerge from under the tea towel with a face like a lobster, only to see Barry grinning down at me. Escape back to Kez's room!

2) We use Kez's Pomegranate Facial Wash for Problem Skin, followed by a Pomegranate Face Mask which we splat on to each other's faces while sitting cross-legged on the bed – this is hilarious and we laugh so much that our face masks, which have dried hard, crack and bits fall off.

3) Sophie has a panic attack – she keeps having them every time she remembers Kez's threat to kill us if we

touch her things. I tell her not to worry – we will tidy up afterwards. Kezia will never know.

4) We wash off the remaining bits of face mask with warm water and Pomegranate Facial Toner, followed by Pomegranate Moisturiser.

5) We depilate. This takes place in the bathroom and involves a can of Smooth Operator depilatory cream and a razor. Sophie shrieks when she cuts herself. Mum storms into the bathroom, clearly stressed (a Total Babes' Night In is meant to be relaxing!). After giving Sophie a sticking plaster, she sends us to bed. Sophie is stressed because she hadn't finished depilating, and she is worried that her admirer will think she's weird when he finds out that she has one smooth leg, and one hairy one . . .

Chapter 4

Sophie

IT'S EASTER MONDAY MORNING and we're in trouble. Kezia has arrived back early *before* Tash and I have had a chance to tidy up! We are on the receiving end of one of Kezia's most thunderous looks!

'I don't believe it!' she explodes. 'What have you done to my room?' Just then Tash's mobile starts chirruping. 'And which of you complete morons is

EXAMPLE OF ONE OF KEZIA'S THUNDEROUS LOOKS

responsible for that STUPID ringtone?'

'It's my new ringtone,' Tash replies. 'And it's really cool. It's called the Crazy Cuckoo – everyone's got it! It was meant to go off in time to wake us up to tidy your room, but you beat us to it.'

'It is the single most IRRITATING thing I have EVER heard!' Kezia bellows. 'And how can two people make so much mess? Look at all those clothes all over the floor, and toenail clippings – yeuk! Gross!'

Kezia walks over to the shelf where she keeps all her pomegranate stuff, which is now scattered round the room. I start whimpering . . . I can't help it!

'You little . . .!' she begins. 'Have you *any* idea how much this stuff costs? Are you completely brain dead? Are you . . .?'

'Why's it such a big deal?' Tash shouts. 'Why are you always so grumpy? We're going to be Alfie's godparents next weekend – do you really think he wants godparents who are always shouting at each other?'

'Er – I happen to have brought over a special set of calming stones,' I stammer. 'They're aventurines. You lie on your front and I place the stones on your back and you feel calm and relaxed – it's simple! Shall we give it a go?' I fish the smooth pale green stones – one large, one medium, one small – out of my pocket and lay them on Kezia's bed. But Kezia seems more interested in examining a small patch of carpet . . .

CALMING STONES

'Blue paint!' she roars. 'You have got blue paint on my carpet! AND bits of face pack! So I am officially throwing you out! Go on – out! I've had enough!'

'I hate it when she shouts like that,' says Tash, stirring the paint. 'It reminds me of when Mum and Dad used to shout, before they got divorced. AND I've got a cold – she should be nice to me!'

'But she's not always like that,' I point out. 'Remember the Midnight Feast of Chocolate? She was so nice and friendly.'

'I know – she *can* be nice. I wish she was like that all the time. She doesn't realise how lucky she is. She's allowed a television AND Geoffrey in her room – he'll be back later, by the way.'

'And she's got you for a sister – so I think she's lucky,' I say.

'Thanks, Sofe!'

We are back in Tash's room, covering up more green. Wave upon wave of Skydance Blue rolls across the walls. 'We'll have this finished soon,' I remark. 'Then we can paint the skirting-board and put up the border. It's going to match your duvet perfectly – I think you're going to have the coolest room in the whole house, Tash!'

'Yes,' Tash agrees. 'Kezia's welcome to her stupid green carpet! Ouch! I shouldn't have blown my nose just now, it's made that horrid pimple on my nose hurt even more! All that steaming for nothing! I want it to go in time for the christening – so I'm giving up chocolate and I'm going to *think* my skin clear! I'm going to think pure, chocolate-free thoughts.'

'I'll join you,' I say. 'I've eaten far too much chocolate recently – it's time to have another go at that Resolution To Give Up Chocolate which we made last year – remember? Because I'm not feeling any more like a Total Babe at the moment, even after all those beauty treatments! So I'm not going to think about chocolate OR about Luke – my thoughts about Luke are *not* pure . . . Oh no! I'm thinking about him NOW! It was Luke's fault I didn't keep the Resolution last time – he drove me to chocolate! I felt I couldn't live without Luke AND without chocolate!

'So don't let him make you feel like that again. If it *is* him writing those poems and things, he's probably just playing with your feelings – that's what he's like.

Sophie! You're *not* thinking of getting back together with Luke, are you?'

'I don't really know *what* to think at the moment, Tash – because I don't know who it is! I don't know whether to keep the poems forever, like Granny did, or put them straight in the bin! I don't KNOW!'

'OK, Sofe – calm down! Perhaps Inspector Kyle will solve the mystery soon – let's hope so! Shall we go for a walk? The paint fumes are making me feel strange. Can I stay at your house tonight now that we've been booted out by Kezia? Your parents are so nice and normal compared to my weird family. And talking to Dad has made me feel even less like being around Barry . . .'

I am finding it hard to relax and enjoy my walk in the park with Tash because of the feeling that every bush and tree we pass might conceal an anonymous poet staring at me, longing for me, palely loitering, sighing, yearning . . . I try to think pure thoughts . . . pure, clear water . . . pure, melting chocolate . . .

'Hi!' says a voice just behind us.

'Aaargh!' I shriek, doing a little leap into the air. My stomach cartwheels into my throat.

'Sorry!' says the voice. 'Didn't mean to make you jump!'

Turning round I am confronted by Luke and Lydia, their arms entwined around each others' waists, grinning at me. I feel myself going into Full Tomato Mode – my face is burning!

Rob is also there with a sporty girl called Sandi who captains the St Boris's Girls' First Eleven Hockey Team.

ROB AND SANDI   AND LUKE AND LYDIA

Tash has half turned away from everyone and I realise that she is trying to conceal her nose and has her hand raised to her face . . .

'So are you two coming to my party next week?' Lydia asks, her Bambi-esque lashes almost touching her nose – I hate her!

'We might,' I reply, trying to sound cool and casual. My voice has gone croaky.

'There's going to be a disco, a bouncy castle, a conjuror

and stilt-walkers and a living statue and . . . and everything!' Lydia gushes. 'It's going to be like a little kid's party – in an ironic and totally cool way, of course! My dad's got this huge double garage on the side of the house, and I'm having the party in there – minus the cars, of course – they might get in the way!'

There is a strange braying noise which I realise is Sandi laughing . . .

'So what's new?' Luke asks me.

'Oh – nothing much,' I reply. 'Eat, sleep, eat, sleep – you know, the usual,' I say, but I have a sudden urge to make Luke jealous and make him realise what he's missing! 'Oh – and I've got a secret admirer,' I say, casually. 'Someone's writing me love poems.'

'Really?' exclaims Luke, his eyes widening. 'What kind of sad freak would do that?'

This is not quite the reaction I was looking for.

'Seriously weird!' barks Sandi in a surprisingly deep voice.

I feel like saying 'Who asked *you*?' I am sure that no one will ever write *her* a love poem . . .

Rob hasn't said a word. He is staring at his feet.

'Ah . . . ah . . . ah . . . AH . . . TISHOOOO!!!' Tash sneezes resoundingly, and a shiny glob of snot shoots straight on to the toe of Rob's left trainer, just where he is staring. Everyone looks at it.

I can feel Tash freeze beside me – 'Hide me!' she

chokes – and I know I have to get her back to my house immediately for some intensive calming treatments . . .

'I crashed, burned AND imploded!' Tash moans. 'I can never go out in public again – ever! I must shut myself away! I must . . .'

'TASH! It really wasn't that bad!' I plead with her. We are perched on the edge of my bed in the middle of my half-painted room.

'Not that bad?' Tash shrieks – I tell her to keep her voice down. 'It was worse!' she continues, in a strangled tone. 'I didn't know I was going to feel like that about Rob until I saw him with someone else – and then I snotted all over his shoe.'

... AND THEN I SNOTTED ALL OVER HIS SHOE!

'You're exaggerating – it was only a little piece of snot.'
I am now sitting cross-legged on my bed doing unflattering drawings in my sketchbook of Lydia and Sandi – they are both as bad as each other, in my opinion.

'But he was staring straight at it!' Tash groans. 'It's like someone just stuck a pin into the balloon of my potential cool – in fact, it's more like someone attacked it with a chainsaw! Oh – I couldn't feel any *less* like a Total Babe – it was a total NON-Total Babe moment! And you know what the really stupid thing is? I didn't care when he was only going out with his bike . . .'

'But Sandi's awful! She's always saying things behind people's backs in that deep, husky voice of hers – I think *she* thinks it's sexy! And Rob was really unkind to you when you hurt yourself and he only cared about his bike – surely you don't want him back?'

'Oh – I don't know! I'm just upset because he's with someone and I'm on my own. I don't think I want him back *really* – I'm just confused . . .'

'Me too! I don't want Luke back – at least I don't think I do. I think I just want to eat chocolate . . .'

'Sophie – no! Chocolate is not the answer!' Tash cries. 'We must get back to the Total Babe regime – I need an emergency makeover – or a Total Babe whole body transplant, or something! Then she sees the chocolate bunnies in my room. 'Or maybe it is . . .'

'Yes – just the ears off those chocolate bunnies?

Our Resolution To Give Up Chocolate starts from tomorrow!'

'Oh – go on, then! Give me one! And let's have some music,' says Tash.

Forgotten Girl sounds echoey without the curtains in the windows.

'Luke can't possibly be the poet,' I remark. 'It wouldn't make sense – would it?' I feel devastated by what just happened – it was sooo humiliating to be made to feel like an idiot in front of Luke and Lydia. My own fault, of course, for mentioning my secret admirer – I should have kept him *secret*! What if Luke tells people about this at school – he might frighten my shy guy away! Or was Luke just being defensive and trying to cover up the fact that it was him? But it can't be – can it? I ask Tash the same question again.

She shakes her head hopelessly.

'Oh – let's get on with the painting!' I suggest. 'At least that makes sense, and it will help to take your mind off the fact that you snotted on Rob's shoe.'

Tash emits a low moan. But I'm sure she must be glad to have me around to cheer her up. This is what Best Mates do – and thinking about Tash helps to take my mind off my own problems . . .

Chapter 5

Natasha

'TOTAL PAINTORAMA!' I enthuse, gazing at the blue walls of Sophie's new-look bedroom. I am glad that we chose this colour, since the green that used to cover the walls of my own room now reminds me of snot . . . We stayed up late last night painting, and heard Kyle getting a huge telling-off for coming home nearly two hours after the agreed time. I am feeling better about the whole snot incident after spending quality BMF time with Sophie – she is good at cheering me up. I still have a cold, but it is not a heavy one.

Sophie's mum made us go to bed in the spare room, and I had a disturbed night, having strange dreams about Mum, Barry and snot. This morning Sophie's mum brought us cups of tea, and we are now standing in Sophie's room, wrapped in our duvets, cups of tea in our hands. (We have agreed that tea counts towards the three litres of water we are meant to be drinking per day.)

'I love my room!' says Sophie. 'And Mum said what a wonderful job we'd done – she's even given us ten pounds to catch the bus into Bodmington later and enjoy ourselves. So we'll hit the town and get face packs, hair conditioner, depilatory cream and all the other stuff we need to be Total Babes!'

'Your parents are so warm and welcoming,' I say. At this precise moment we hear Sophie's mum yelling.

'Get out! Get out! Get out of this house – and don't come back! Go on – shoo!'

'Oh my God!' Sophie exclaims. 'Mum's throwing Dad out of the house!'

'I don't think so, Sofe . . .'

We shuffle downstairs, still wrapped in our duvets, and find Sophie's mum on her hands and knees scrubbing the living-room carpet where Twizzler has recently thrown up.

'I'm fed up with that cat coming into the house!' she exclaims.

'Mum,' Sophie says, 'is Kyle grounded?'

'Only for the next ten years,' she says, scrubbing the carpet.

'It's just that Tash and I would really like him to come into Bodmington with us – it *is* the holidays, after all.'

This is news to me! Why on earth does Sophie want her little brother tagging along? All he does is ogle the latest games in boring shops . . .

Sophie's mum sighs. 'He can go into Bodmington with you – but he must stay in during the evenings.'

When I ask her, Sophie explains that she read in *Allure* magazine that charity shops are great places for finding great clothes at crazily cheap prices, and she wants us all to go to one and get properly kitted out as Total Babes and Babe Magnets. And she wants Kyle to continue with his investigations into the identity of her admirer, so we can all go to Froth's Coffeehouse afterwards where a lot of people from our Year hang out.

Kyle does not seem thrilled by our plan to transform his fashion sense.

'Isn't this better than being stuck at home in your room?' Sophie asks, placing a trilby hat on his head and adjusting it to the right angle. We are in the Care for the Aged charity shop, which does not strike me as the best place to turn ourselves into Total Babes.

'VERY Inspector Kyle!' Sophie enthuses, stepping back to admire the hat. 'It's only forty pence!'

'It smells,' says Kyle, grumpily. 'And I'll get hat hair.'

'Well – if you can't be *bothered* to show any enthusiasm!' Sophie snaps. 'I'll help Tash, instead!'

Oh no.

By the time we leave Care for the Aged, Sophie, in her new role as fashion adviser, has failed to persuade me to wear a floppy-brimmed, off-white hippy hat . . .

'It is sooo you, Tash!'

'It is sooo NOT.'

She has also failed to persuade Kyle to wear a dodgy-looking fake leather jacket . . .

'It makes me look gay,' he says. 'Exactly how is that going to impress Jolene?'

With a despairing gesture, Sophie turns away from both of us and rummages through the rails of clothes, acquiring a faded denim jacket which she wears with the hippy hat I rejected.

'Very boho,' she says, as we leave the shop. 'And all for a pound! I'm glad you let me buy you those love beads, Tash – only twenty pence! Love beads are sooo . . . lovely.'

'Very oh no!' I think to myself, silently cursing *Allure* magazine. I want to take off the love beads which aren't

VERY BOHO!

VERY OH NO...

really my sort of thing – but I don't want to offend Sophie!

Kyle, who hates shopping, actually shows enthusiasm when Sophie offers to buy him some body spray – it turns out that he knows exactly which one he wants . . .

'Don't tell me you've been reading *Allure* magazine as well?' Sophie asks him. 'That article about the ten best body sprays? So you've been in my room AGAIN!'

Kyle blushes. 'No!' he protests. 'It was my own idea – honestly! I am trying . . .' he adds.

'I *know* you're trying!' Sophie teases, paying for the Total Sex God body spray. Kyle immediately sprays himself all over with it, and Sophie and I start coughing. It is strong but not unpleasant . . .

'Remember – less is more, Kyle!' Sophie gasps. 'Use it in moderation – you don't want to overwhelm Jolene!'

We have just enough money left to go to Froth's Coffeehouse in the mall. Jolene has texted Kyle to say that she might meet him there.

Froth's is packed with people from our Year and above, as usual. Sophie reminds Kyle that another reason for wanting him to come along today was so that he could find more clues to the identity of her secret admirer.

We find a table and order three Easter Specials – a mocha which arrives under a heap of whipped cream, mini marshmallows, chocolate shavings and a cinnamon stick. Our Resolution To Give Up Chocolate starts from tomorrow! For sure! Sophie says that hot chocolate or mocha is a drink and therefore doesn't count . . .

'Sofe!' I whisper. 'Look over there! It's James! He's clearing tables – he must be working here.' Oooh! I suddenly realise how much I fancy him – he has a cute smile, deep brown eyes, cool hair – I don't know how I'm going to cope if he turns out to be Sophie's secret admirer!

Inspector Kyle is suddenly alert, his eyes trained on James. As he passes by our table, Kyle calls out to him: 'Hi, James! I've got two serious CHOCOHOLICS here!'

James smiles. 'Be with you in a minute!' he calls back.

'Did you see that?' Kyle hisses at us. 'He reacted to the word "chocoholic"!'

'Yes, Kyle,' says Sophie, slowly. 'You talked to him – of course he reacted!'

'But he smiled at you! It *might* be him – he might have left the chocolates!'

'He smiled at all of us,' says Sophie – but she can't help looking hopeful.

I can't help wishing that it was just *me* who James was smiling at – or perhaps he was merely amused by Sophie's hat!

A few minutes later, Jolene enters the coffee shop, sees Kyle and joins us. 'What IS that smell?' she exclaims, pulling up a chair. 'Oh! It's *you*, Kyle! It's – er – different . . .' Jolene is small, slim and blonde, with a friendly peachy-skinned face and a big smile. She is wearing low-slung hipster jeans and a wide belt, and carries a small white handbag. She tells Sophie that she really likes her hat! Kyle smiles at her, leans back in his chair and emits a loud burp. Jolene doesn't seem to mind, but I am appalled – has he learned *nothing*?!

James is now clearing a table quite close to where we are sitting.

JOLENE

Sophie clears her voice. 'Ahem – I lurve poetry, don't you, Tash?' she says loudly, fixing me with a look – she has either developed a nervous twitch or she is trying to wink at me. 'Poetry is sooo romantic, don't you think?' she continues. 'I like to read it while I am eating chocolates! Yes! I really love POETRY!' She almost shouts the last word as James is now walking away from us with a tray of used cups and plates. I feel deeply embarrassed! Sophie can be a bit too obvious – perhaps James will go for someone more subtle, like me . . .

Jolene looks at Sophie and then at Kyle as if to say: You didn't tell me that your sister was completely mad.

The next time James passes our table, he stops, looks

at Sophie strangely and shakes his head. She doesn't notice this as she cannot see him from under the brim of her hat. Then he smiles at *me*! My heart leaps! Suddenly Sophie looks up, sees James and flashes him her most radiant smile.

'Yesss!!!' she exclaims, when James is out of earshot again. 'It *must* be him – why else would he look nervous like that?'

'I think you made him nervous,' I say. I feel profoundly irritated. Sophie has never expressed a serious interest in James until now, whereas I have worshipped him from afar for ages. I am even more annoyed when Sophie pretends she needs to go to the women's toilets *just* so that she can walk past James and do her sexy bottom wiggle. But I think it is a mistake – she still looks like a duck!

I can't help hoping that Sophie's secret admirer turns out to be Nerd of the Year, a.k.a. Ed. Then she'll go off the whole idea and we can go back to being BMF without boyfriends. I think this is better than one of us – Sophie – having a boyfriend, and the other one – me – not having a boyfriend. But then James really did smile at me. Does that mean he fancies me? Or was he smiling out of sympathy because I have a mad friend? But am I being too harsh on Sophie? Would I act the same as her if James decided to pursue me, and Sophie was left on her own?

I must stop being so self-centred! I should be feeling glad for Sophie for having a secret admirer – I know it's really romantic . . . But it's not easy seeing everyone pairing up – Rob and Sandi (particularly), Luke and Lydia, Kyle and Jolene, Sophie and her Babe of Destiny – and knowing that I could soon be left out in the cold WITH a cold and only the spot on the end of my nose for company. Everyone has someone except me – Kezia has her boyfriend Geoffrey and Mum has Barry . . .

I wish I could be a Total Babe like Sophie and then I could have a secret admirer too, such as . . . James! He *did* smile at me, but I think he smiled at Sophie differently – probably because he fancies her and is *her* secret admirer. Am I just unlucky? Perhaps I haven't met the right person yet – someone who will see through my Non-Total Babe exterior to the real me? Or is there still a chance that I *can* transform myself into a Total Babe? I don't know . . .

Blip! Blip! Beeeeep!

I have a message on my phone. It's from Dad! SEE YOU SOON! It's almost as if he knew I was feeling down and sent me a message just at the right moment to cheer me up!

Sophie spends the whole of the bus journey home raving about how she and James are obviously meant to BE, and how drop-dead gorgeous he is and how his bum scores ten on the Sophie Scale etc. etc. She is fizzing like a firework fuse, and I decide not to rain on her picnic by mentioning the possibility that it could be Ed or one of the other boys in the French group . . . I have to make quite an effort as she is beginning to annoy me.

Kyle is bringing Jolene home to meet the family. I think he is incredibly brave, knowing from experience how embarrassingly parents can behave when they are around your friends – I think they like to show off. But it is a compliment to Jolene that he wants to introduce her. He doesn't mention to her that he also wants her to come to the house because he is grounded in the evenings and wouldn't be able to see her otherwise.

'I think you're mad, Kyle!' says Sophie jokily as we walk from the bus stop in Southway Central back to Sophie's house. 'I'm not going to risk bringing James within a hundred kilometres of Mum and Dad in case Mum brings out the baby photos of me lying naked on a rug and that mega-embarrassing one of the first time I used the potty successfully, and . . . what . . . the . . . I mean . . . who . . . is . . . *that*?'

Sophie's voice has gone into slow motion and sunk to little more than a whisper. We have reached the garden gate and there is someone – a teenage boy – pushing something through Sophie's letterbox. He has his back to us so I can't see who it is.

'Quick! Duck down! Don't let him see us!' hisses

Inspector Kyle, taking charge. We all duck down behind the hedge.

'Leave this to me!' says Kyle. 'Stay where you are!' He gets up and confronts the boy who is now walking towards us down the path.

'Oh – hi there, mate!' says the boy. 'Where did you come from – I'm sure you weren't there a moment ago.'

It is a tall, slim boy called Will – from the French group.

'It's not James!' whispers Sophie at my elbow – she sounds surprised and slightly disappointed. 'But he's not bad-looking! In fact, as anonymous admirers go, he's OK! He'll do. My Babe of Destiny! My tall, dark stranger!'

'Ssh!' I hiss. 'Let's listen!'

'I think we need to have a word,' says Kyle, blocking the path so that Will can't get past.

'Sure. What is it, mate?' Will sounds taken aback. 'Your name's Kyle, right? Your sister's in my French group.'

'Aha! You admit it!'

'Eh? Hang on, mate – why would I deny it?'

'Don't you think it would have been better to talk to her about how you feel instead of sending her all those love poems and stuff?' says Kyle. 'She's driving us all mad – and it's your fault!'

WILL

Will scratches the side of his head. 'Er, look, mate, no offence or anything, but I really don't fancy your sister.'

Sophie gives a muffled squeak beside me. I can feel a sneeze building up inside my nose.

'Besides, I'm dyslexic. Poetry isn't really my thing, mate. I'm more into boxing . . .'

Sophie has buried her face in her hands.

Kyle looks behind him nervously, and licks his lips which have obviously gone suddenly dry.

'So . . . so . . . what did you just push through the letterbox?' he falters.

'Oh – that!' says Will, defensively. 'That was a flyer for Pizza Palace – I work there. Got any objection?'

'Er . . . no!' Kyle stands aside to let Will pass. Suddenly I let out an explosive sneeze. Will stares in our direction as, slowly, Sophie, Jolene and I all stand up from where we have been hiding behind the hedge.

Will gives us a long hard look. 'You're all nutters!' he says, before wandering away, shaking his head.

'He said he didn't fancy me!' wails Sophie, upstairs in her room, where we are all sitting amongst the decorating clutter, trying to chill after what was quite frankly a weird experience. Her parents are not at home – they must have gone shopping, stocking up again after Easter. 'Do you realise – this is going to be *all over* school next term? Everyone's going to be laughing at me!' she wails. 'And it's all YOUR fault, Kyle! You can forget all that Inspector Kyle rubbish – you're fired!'

'Steady on, Sofe!' I say. 'It was an honest mistake.'

'Yes, I was only trying to help!' Kyle protests. 'But I don't really care any more – you can do your own detective work in future. I resign! Come on, Jolene – let's go!'

Moments later I hear Sophie's mum and dad getting back. Sophie's mum does that little trilling laugh which she only does when there are guests.

'So good to meet you at last, Charlene!' I hear her say. 'We've heard so much about you!' (I'm sure Kyle's never mentioned her to his parents before . . .) 'Only good things, of course.' Trill, trill.

'Her name's Jolene, Mum.' (I can hear the note of panic in Kyle's voice.)

'I'm just about to make a nice cup of tea. Come and join us, Gillian. I know! I'll get the photo albums! Kyle was such an *adorable* baby . . .'

'Poor Kyle!' I comment, as I close the bedroom door.

'Serves him right,' snaps Sophie. 'He totally embarrassed me – now it's *his* turn!' She is holding a calming stone, gripping it hard.

'Oh, come on, Sofe! That's unfair! He was looking out for you – you know, doing protective brother stuff.'

'I'm sooooo embarrassed!' moans Sophie, burying

her face in her hands again. 'I may never leave the house – ever!'

'But look on the bright side,' I appeal to her. 'If it's not Will, then it *could* still be James!'

Sophie looks up and her face brightens. 'Ooooh – yes! Strange – I hadn't thought of that! I must have been too upset and embarrassed to think straight! But you're right – thanks, Tash! I feel re-empowered!'

Sophie's sense of re-empowerment means that she goes into motor-mouth mode on the subject of how gorgeous James is. I resort to painting the skirting-board with *Forgotten Girl* turned up loud to drown out the long list Sophie is reeling off of all James's attributes. I agree with her – but I want James for myself, and the yearning is painful. I may have to write a poem . . .

Sophie helps paint the skirting-board. Twizzler comes to join us.

'Oh no!' I exclaim. 'He's just brushed against the paint – now you've got a furry skirting-board and Twizzler's got white streaks!'

We start giggling. Sophie catches hold of Twizzler and we carefully wipe the paint off his fur, snipping off a few strands where it is hard to remove. Then we groom him with Crumpet's dog-brush. Twizzler loves his beauty treatment and purrs his deep rumbling purr. We remove several knots from his coat, and all the twigs and leaves that have got tangled in it.

It feels good to forget about our problems for a while and concentrate on doing enjoyable BMF stuff, such as redecorating, cat-grooming, listening to music – and just being together. We do some Total Babe stuff as well, to make ourselves feel better. We rub in loads of blueberry and damson body lotion – it is supposed to make your skin feel silky, although Sophie complains of feeling 'slimy', which gets us giggling. Even my cold feels a lot better. Sophie goes a whole twenty minutes without mentioning James once! (I distracted her with a chocolate hen. She says her Resolution To Give Up Chocolate starts from tomorrow – I promise to start from tomorrow as well . . .)

Chapter 6
Sophie

'SHOW ME YOUR TONGUE! Now! Out with it!' Tash is standing in front of me in my room, refusing to let me past until I stick out my tongue at her.

'OUT WITH IT!'

'Aaaaah!' I go.

'Hah! I thought so!' Tash exclaims. 'It's all brown. You've been eating chocolate – and it's only ten in the morning! You have *no* willpower, Sophie Edwards! I thought you said the Resolution To Give Up Chocolate began today. Because it didn't begin yesterday. Or the day before.'

'It takes a while to get going. And I've been feeling stressed because I haven't received any poems recently – I hope something or someone hasn't put him off!'

'I doubt it,' says Tash. 'And failing to receive a love poem for three or four days in a row is no excuse for breaking all your resolutions. What about eating fruit and veg and drinking three litres of water a day?'

FRUIT AND VEG AND THREE LITRES OF WATER

'I'm doing that – why did you think I was up all night going to the loo?'

It is Thursday morning. We spent yesterday flitting between my house and Tash's, putting the final touches on our rooms. They are nearly finished, and they look good. Tash's mum was so impressed that she has offered to pay us to paint some other rooms in her house – she says that she is sick of green too! Even Kezia said that she liked what we've done – she seems to have calmed down a lot now that Geoffrey is back, and she told us that the paint came off her carpet quite easily. She said she was sorry for being so grumpy while we were sharing her room, and told us how much she is looking forward to the christening. She even asked Tash to play the Crazy Cuckoo ringtone so that Geoffrey could hear it!

CRAZY CUCKOO

'We can start moving stuff back into place against the walls,' I remark, gazing at my room in all its blueness. 'There's just one part of the skirting-board which is still a bit wet.'

Tash is peering at her nose in a small compact mirror and applying more spot cream. 'I've only got until tomorrow to zap this zit!' she says. 'I don't want it to still be there when I become a godparent. At least my cold doesn't seem too bad now.'

'The spot's nearly gone,' I say, encouragingly. 'Keep drinking loads of water so that you flush the toxins and the cold germs out of your system. And if all else fails, you can borrow my spot concealer.'

Tash grabs her water bottle and takes a huge swig, which sucks in its plastic sides. 'By the time I've finished, there won't be a single toxin left in my body!' she exclaims.

We go downstairs. Mum left early this morning to go to work at the library, but Dad is a teacher so he is home for the holidays. He has offered to drive us into Bodmington so that we can go round the shops and Tash can collect the silver piggy bank which is being engraved as a christening gift for Alfie – Tash's mum gave her some money for this, and Kezia made a contribution. Tash has also been given some money to buy a skirt as her mum said she couldn't wear jeans to the christening. I hope my purple dress is OK. I bought it on a recent shopping trip, and Tash really likes it. Mum has given me some money and made me an appointment at A Cut Above to have my hair trimmed ready for the christening. I hope the stylist realises that I am a Total Babe in the making and gives me suitably 'Tip Top Tresses'! Tash is going to get some Anti-Frizz hair conditioner with which to – hopefully – tame her own tresses.

'I hope Mum's cool about all of this christening stuff,' says Tash as we head downstairs.

'Have you talked to her?' I ask.

'No, she's always with Barry. I'll go round later to say goodbye and make sure she's OK.'

'Good idea. Oh – I am *so* looking forward to having my hair cut!' I exclaim. But my voice trails away as I

freeze in the doorway to the living room. Dad is sitting in his favourite armchair, reading a magazine called *Properties in France*. On the coffee table in front of him are a couple of issues of another magazine called *French Property Buyer*. And on the floor by his chair is a stack of still more magazines on the same subject.

'This is bad!' I groan quietly. 'This is very bad! It looks like Dad's still considering moving to France, despite what Mum said. Tash! I don't want to go!'

'I don't want you to go, either. You must resist! What was that idea you mentioned after we had been to Granny's – the one that would put your dad right off the idea of going to France? We got interrupted and you never told me . . .'

'Oh! Thanks for reminding me! But I can't explain now – Dad's seen us.'

'Are you two girls ready to go?' Dad asks, getting up from his chair. 'Good! Let's get in the car.'

* * *

My idea is breathtaking in its simplicity. I have been too busy and too preoccupied with thoughts of being a Total Babe and of anonymous admirers such as James to explain it to Tash so she may be confused at first until she realises what I am doing. Dad is an over-protective parent and my aim is to worry him so much that he will no longer be able to cope with the idea of taking me to France – and the ideal moment to put my cunning plan into action has just arrived.

Tash and I are sitting together in the back of the car with Kyle in the passenger seat beside Dad. Kyle is going to meet Jolene in Bodmington – she survived meeting our family and, surprisingly, does not seem to have been put off!

Taking a deep breath, I make a loud 'Mmmmmmmmm!' sound which makes everyone jump. Tash looks at me with round eyes and shrinks down in her seat, a nervous grin on her face.

Kyle twists round in the passenger seat and gives me a look. 'What's up with you?' he asks.

'Oh – I was just thinking about all those French love gods waiting for me across the Channel!'

'What French love gods?' Kyle asks. 'What are you on about?'

Tash has got the giggles.

'Don't you think that the French have got the most

kissable mouths in the whole universe?' I ask. 'I can't *wait* to lock lips with all those luscious lads with names like Pierre, Jean-Pierre, Philippe, Jean-Philippe, Louis, Jean-Louis, and all the others! I'll never get enough FRENCH KISSING!!!'

Tash's giggles have turned into nervous hysterics – she has never heard me talk like this in front of Dad before – probably because I never have.

Kyle is glaring at me disapprovingly, but I press on – my entire future depends on this!

'Oooooh yes!' I exclaim. 'The French are the BEST kissers! I'll probably get on a French bus or train and go into some of the major towns and cities so that I can work my way through *all* those French boys! So I'll be out LATE every night and I won't have time for my

I WILL BE TOO BUSY ... KISSING FRENCH BOYS!

homework because I'll be too busy KISSING! FRENCH KISSING! KISSING FRENCH BOYS!!!' I add, ramming the message home.

There is a profound silence in the car, broken only by muffled choking noises from Tash, who has stuffed all her fingers in her mouth at once in an effort to stop herself shrieking with laughter.

I catch sight of Kyle and Dad's faces in the rear-view mirror. Kyle has blushed bright red and is staring fixedly out of the window – and Dad appears to be struggling to keep a straight face. This is not the reaction I was looking for.

DAD DOESN'T REACT...

We have reached Bodmington. Dad parks the car in the Market Square car park and tells us to meet him back there in an hour and a half. 'That means you as well, Kyle!' he adds. Dad is going to browse in a bookshop where they serve coffee and also have Internet access and an art gallery.

He has made no reference at all to my outburst in the car – this is very disconcerting. I have to check. 'Er – are you OK, Dad?' I ask.

'Yes – I'm very well! How are you?' he replies, cheerily.

'I'm fine.'

'Good! Well – I'll see you later.' He wanders off.

Tash gives full vent to her pent-up nervous hysterics and staggers around, gasping and clutching her middle.

Kyle is furious. 'Whatever got into you?' he asks. 'Have you any idea how EMBARRASSING that was?'

'I just wanted to put Dad off the idea of moving to France,' I explain. 'I got the idea from Granny. She got put off by a Frenchman. I thought Dad might be put off by the idea of all those French boys with their tongues stuck down my throat.'

'That is so gross!' Kyle exclaims. 'I'm going to meet Jolene – at least she's *normal*.'

I have had my hair trimmed. The girl who cut it kept talking about her brother and how cute he is – I began to think she wanted me to go out with him! She said that she cut his hair and it looks really cool. Then she asked me if I have brothers or sisters, and the conversation moved on to Kyle. I stopped short of describing him as 'cool' . . . Tash waits for me in the hairdresser's and buys some special salon Anti-Frizz hair conditioner. She admires my hair – I decided to keep the same style as I think it suits me. We leave, and go to the jeweller's.

The silver piggy bank is ready, all shiny and new. It has been engraved with Alfie's name and the date of the christening. Tash drops a shiny ten pence piece into it before the shop assistant puts it in its box and giftwraps it.

As we leave the jeweller's, it starts to rain, and people hurry into shops and cafés.

'We could go to Froth's,' Tash suggests.

'Just to get out of the rain,' I add, casually.

'Of course,' says Tash. 'No other reason.' She gets a compact mirror out of her pocket, checks her make-up and applies more spot concealer – she is sooo obvious!

We find a table for two beside the window and sit down. Tash's gaze wanders around the café until her radar eyes lock on to their target – James. I *know* she fancies him, and I feel sorry for her since it is *me* he likes – I think.

My insides are going wheee! at the sight of James. Now he is coming over to our table to clear away all the cups and plates which the last customers left behind – we chose this table carefully.

Now I know why Tash plastered on so much foundation and concealer before we came out – she thinks it looks cool, but the effect is clownish. I'm glad I used only a little light lip-gloss and some blue eyeshadow to enhance my best features, although right now I'd settle for a paper bag to put over my head since I can feel myself blushing full tomato – *why* do I do this? Why can't I think of a single thing to say while James clears our table? Tash and I sit like shop dummies in stony silence staring at the table in front of us. Quick! Quick! Think of *something* to say – ANYTHING!

'I've got a terrible criv . . .' I say. James and Tash both look at me.

'I've got a terrible criv . . .' I begin again.

James hesitates, holding his tray of dirty cups and plates – then he heads off in the direction of the kitchen.

'Would you mind explaining,' says Tash. 'What is a "terrible criv"?'

I let out a low groan of despair. 'I *wanted* to say: "I've got a terrible craving for chocolate!"' I explain. 'It was the *only* thing I could think of to say – and I wanted to say *something*. But it kept coming out wrong! I can say it perfectly now that James has gone! He must think I'm a complete idiot.'

'Oh look, the sun's coming out,' remarks Tash. (Nice of her to reassure me that James doesn't think I'm a complete idiot . . .)

'I don't think I want anything to drink,' I say. 'Shall we just go?'

'I thought you had a terrible criv?' she asks, innocently.

'Shut up.'

If I didn't know Tash better – and she is my BMF, after

all – I would say that she is pleased that I just made a total fool of myself in front of James . . .

By the time we get home, having bought Tash a plain black skirt and then found Kyle, who was with Jolene and had lost track of the time, Mum is back from the library. She has something in her hand which she holds out to me.

'I don't know what this is,' she says. 'I found it lying on the doorstep when I got home just now – it's addressed to you.'

My heart performs a little backflip and my stomach does a slow cartwheel as Mum hands me a small parcel wrapped up in yellow tissue paper. There is a label with my name on it – and a single kiss – nothing else.

'Do you have a secret admirer?' Mum asks. I can tell she is about to start trilling.

'Yes – actually I do,' I reply, truthfully. With trembling fingers I pull apart the thin layers of tissue paper to reveal a . . . cool blue rubber wristband. It is an unusual one, with strips of lighter and darker blue. I put it on.

Mum wants to know who my secret admirer is – patiently I explain that if I knew who he was, he wouldn't be secret.

'It can't be James,' says Tash. 'He would have had to be in two places at once – how could he have been clearing tables at Froth's AND leaving a present on your doorstep at the same time?'

'He might have got someone to deliver it for him,' I suggest, desperately. I don't want to give up the idea that it *might* be James . . .

Mum switches into Intensive Parental Questioning Mode:

1) What's been going on?
2) Why didn't I tell her sooner?
3) What exactly has this boy been sending me?
4) Am I sure it's someone from school?
5) Have I been visiting any Internet chat rooms?
6) I *would* tell her, wouldn't I – if there was anything funny going on?
7) And is that the truth?
8) And where do I think I'm going?

Now I know why I didn't tell her sooner! Too many questions! I can do without pressure from the parentals.

Dad has just whispered something in Mum's ear. I catch the words 'car' and 'French' – I feel jittery! Has my cunning plan worked – or has it backfired?

'Come back here, please!' says Mum. 'And sit down. Your father and I wish to have a little chat with you. Kyle, you can stay, too – this concerns you as well.'

'Can Tash stay?' I ask, noticing Tash edging towards the door.

'Yes, if she likes. This won't take too long – but it's very important.' Mum takes a deep breath. 'Have you studied reproduction at school?' she asks.

'You mean sex?' I say.

'Yes.'

'Of course we have! Can we go now?' I *so* don't feel comfortable with Mum talking about this! Argh! I must escape!

'No. Sit down. At your age you start having . . .'

She pauses. Periods? Spots? Mood swings? Premenstrual tension? Facial hair? Body hair? All of the above?

'Urges.'

Urges!

A longer pause.

'It is very important that you think carefully before you act on these urges,' Mum says. 'You may not be ready. When you are sure you are ready, you must take proper precautions or you could become pregnant or catch a sexually transmitted disease – or worse.'

'Your mother's right,' says Dad.

'OK,' I say, squirming in my seat and trying not to look at either Tash or Kyle. 'So can we go now?'

'Yes.'

Mum and Dad look tired. I wonder if I should offer to

make them a nice cup of tea – but I want to escape!

'Embarrassing, or what?' says Kyle as we go upstairs to our rooms. 'What is the matter with this family today? I'm not going to risk bringing Jolene here again! It's a madhouse!' He disappears into his room, muttering.

'I don't think I've put Mum or Dad off the idea of moving to France,' I say to Tash, dispiritedly. 'All I've done is make sure they're too worried to let me out ANYWHERE! And I *wish* I hadn't told them about my secret admirer – they made it seem like something worrying and possibly dodgy – why do they have to trample on my dreams? I'm glad you're here, Tash – I think you're the only one who really understands how I feel!'

I drown my sorrows in a whole litre and a half of water to make up for the chocolate hen I ate earlier – trust Tash to guess what I'd been doing in the bathroom! – and the six mini-eggs I ate just now to console myself. My Resolution To Give Up Chocolate *will* begin tomorrow! Tash retires to the bathroom to pile on the Anti-Frizz conditioner, and reappears with her hair wrapped in a towel, turban-style.

'It says to leave it on for twenty minutes for maximum effect,' she says. 'So I'm going to leave it on for *thirty* minutes!'

An excited Kyle suddenly bursts into my room. 'I've got

a moustache!' he exclaims, his earlier embarrassment apparently forgotten.

Tash and I peer closely at his top lip. I count seven darkish downy hairs, only faintly visible, which is why we haven't noticed them before.

'Bum fluff!' I exclaim.

'You're going to have to start shaving,' says Tash, seriously.

'I feel so much more mature!' Kyle exclaims. Then he clears his voice and says it again, in a deeper voice. 'Aunty Aggie explained all about it in that booklet in last month's *Lurve* magazine.'

'Which you could only have got from my room,' I say in a faintly sarcastic voice. 'You have incriminated yourself! You're not the only one who's good at finding clues, little moustachioed brother!'

Chapter 7

Natasha

APRIL FOOL'S DAY! And my spot has gone! My cold seems to have dried up to little more than the occasional sniff. All the nagging from Sophie for me to drink more and MORE water seems to have worked – although I am seriously sloshing about inside . . .

I am at home, packing to go to Dad's. Sophie stayed at her house last night and I stayed here. Barry was in the kitchen cooking for most of the evening – he is a good cook and makes delicious spaghetti bolognese –

SPAG BOL À LE BARRY
NB/ French is not my best subject!
Sophie x

so I was able to have a chat with Mum, who told me she would be thinking of me on Sunday when I become Alfie's godparent. I asked her if she was OK, and she said yes. It wasn't a long conversation, but she put her arm around me and I felt happy just sitting with her for a while.

Kezia tells me that she has phoned Dad to say that we will be at his house at teatime – so there is no rush to get ready. I have the morning . . .

Sophie arrives in my room with her backpack – she is also carrying Crumpet's dog-brush. I notice that she is wearing her blue wristband.

'We need to return Crumpet's brush!' she says. 'Oh – and I've had the BEST idea for an April Fool to play on Kyle!'

On the way to Granny's house Sophie shows me a blank postcard on which she has stuck an unflattering photo of Kyle, taken in a photo booth when he was mucking about with his mates. Under the photo Sophie has written Brother for Sale in bold black capitals.

'I'm going to ask Mr Singh if he'll stick it up on the Minimart noticeboard!' Sophie giggles. As we are just passing the Joyful Shopper Minimart we decide to go there first. But Mr Singh throws up his hands and refuses to accept the Brother For Sale advertisement.

'I am sorry but I just cannot agree to display your

advertisement on the noticeboard,' he says, shaking his head. 'I think it is morally wrong to attempt to sell your brother.'

We leave.

'I don't think Mr Singh has a sense of humour,' Sophie whispers to me. 'Or maybe he doesn't have a brother . . . Talking of which, there's Kyle! Hi, Kyle! What have you got in your hand?'

Kyle tries to hide whatever it is behind his back, but Sophie manages to snatch it from him. It is a rubbery fake frog which he was no doubt going to drop down the back of her top, like he has done so many times before.

'Yes, Kyle – very mature AND original!' Sophie comments, in tones of withering sarcasm.

'That's the trouble with girls!' Kyle retorts. 'No sense of humour! I must say, I haven't found much to laugh at in your . . . er . . .!'

'In my *what*, Kyle?'

'In your . . . in your MIND!' he retorts.

'He's acting weird,' Sophie remarks, as Kyle scurries away. 'Why?'

'Because he's in love?' I suggest.

'Maybe . . .' says Sophie.

When we get back from Granny's I give Mum the *biggest* hug before we leave, and tell her that I will be thinking of her. Then we stuff our bags in the boot and pile into Kezia's car. I hope it doesn't break down on the way – it's so old and decrepit! Geoffrey isn't coming because he has a lot of work he needs to get on with.

The journey to Dad's house in Eastbury is fun. We sing along to Kezia's *Power Ballads* CD at the top of our voices! We have to stop several times to buy petrol, water, sandwiches, and to go to the loo. Sophie and I are still aiming to drink at least three litres of water per day . . .

Then Sophie goes all quiet.

'Are you OK, Sofe?'

She nods.

'Still wondering who's sending you these things?' I ask.

She nods again, fiddling with the blue wristband. 'Yes – and I'm missing him already. It's weird – missing someone when you don't even know who it is! But I feel the pain of his hopeless longing, and I really want us to be together. Unless it's Ed, of course. But I *really* want to find out who it is before Lydia's party on Tuesday. I'm waiting for Kyle to text me – I want him to send me regular updates on anything he's managed to find out – and I want updates on Mum and Dad's strange obsession with France.'

'I thought Kyle was sacked. And then he resigned as well.'

'He'll do it – especially if I bribe him. I texted him a

while ago saying that he can have my sound system when I get the new one I'm saving up for. And he can even borrow it before that, when Jolene comes round. He really likes my sound system – his own is all clapped-out – I think that awful music he listens to killed it . . . Ah! I thought so. Here's a reply message – he's agreed to send regular reports.'

'And are you sure you're not worried about anything else?' I ask. 'I mean – you're not nervous about going to stay with Dad and his new family, are you?'

'Of course not! As long as I'm with you, and you're OK, I've got no reason to be nervous, have I? It's ages since I saw your Dad – I'm really looking forward to seeing him again – I remember when he used to take us for rides in a wheelbarrow.'

'Oh yes! I remember! Oh my God – we must have been so tiny!' I feel very glad that I have Sophie to share these happy memories with.

Reaching into my pocket I pull out a folded piece of paper. 'Don't worry!' I say, noticing the expression on Sophie's face. 'It's not a love poem from an anonymous poet! It's a list I made of things you ought to be prepared for when you go to stay at my dad's – forewarned is forearmed, as they say!'

Sophie takes the sheet of paper and reads:

Nice Things About Staying at my Dad's	Cringe-making Things About Staying at my Dad's
1) Going shopping in Ditchfield and ogling the gorgeous assistant in Grip.	1) Dad and Wendy's habit of calling each other Tweetypie and Plumcake (cringe!).
2) Dad's delicious shepherd's pie.	2) Dad and Wendy's habit of walking round the house in very short His and Hers white towelling dressing gowns.
3) Alfie.	3) Alfie's nappies
4) Wendy's collection of surprisingly cool CDs which she doesn't mind me listening to on her Walkman if I've forgotten to bring my own.	4) Dad's habit of singing in the bath.

'I could go on – but you probably get the picture!' I say.

'That's fine, it sounds a lot of fun!'

'Oh, and don't blink when we get to Eastbury or you'll miss it. There's not much there apart from one street, one shop, a handful of houses, a couple of ducks on a very small pond at the end of the street, and the beardie-weirdie who seems to live in the bus shelter – Dad says he's harmless . . .'

Sophie doesn't notice Eastbury at all as she is distracted by a text from Kyle to say that there is someone lurking in the bushes outside their house! She immediately starts to panic until a second text from Kyle arrives to say that the 'someone in the bushes' turned out to be Twizzler. Sophie texts back to tell him not to bother texting her until he has something even remotely sensible to say . . .

We are all sitting around the kitchen table in Dad's house eating shepherd's pie. Alfie is squealing with delight. I feel completely at home, and Sophie looks happy, too.

Suddenly I realise that I am glad that Mum has Barry to keep her company and even cook for her – it wouldn't have been very nice for her to be all on her own while we were here enjoying ourselves. I feel pleased that I have had an unselfish thought!

After supper I have a little chat with Dad about Mum and Barry. He agrees with me that it is a good thing that

Mum isn't lonely – he tells me that he met Barry a long time ago, and liked him. This immediately makes me feel better. Barry must be OK, if Dad likes him. Dad also reassures me that it is natural for me to feel jealous from time to time if Mum is spending a lot of her time with Barry. He suggests that I ask Mum to take me on a shopping trip sometime so that we can spend some 'quality time' together.

'Did someone mention "shopping"?' says Wendy, emerging from behind her magazine. Alfie is on the floor at her feet, playing with his toys until his bedtime – and Sophie is down on the carpet, too, playing a little car game with him. Kezia has gone to have a bath.

Dad laughs. 'So who'd like to go into Ditchfield tomorrow morning?'

We all chorus 'Yes!'

'That's settled then,' he says.

Before I go to sleep I text Mum: LOVE YOU!

Sophie has already phoned home to tell her parents that she has arrived safely, and to ask her mum to remind Kyle to stay out of her room IF he wants her sound system!

'I like it here!' she says. 'This bed is sooo comfortable!' Sophie and I are in the double bed in the spare room, and Kezia is nearby on an inflatable mattress. She said that she was happy for Sophie and me to have the bed. She is being really kind – I think she felt guilty about before. This time there is no arguing, yelling or grumbling.

'I thought about what you said, Tash,' says Kezia. 'And I agree with you – Alfie doesn't need godparents who are always arguing – he deserves the *best* godparents.'

'And we're going to be the best,' I say, sleepily, as the clock on the landing ticks gently . . .

Sophie sighs. 'It's so peaceful,' she says. 'Apart from the torment in my soul – the longing to be united at last with the one who adores me. I wonder if he's sent me any more poems or gifts.'

'I'm sure Kyle would let you know, Sofe,' I say.

'Yes – he *really* wants my sound system, so he'll be doing everything he can, I'm sure of that.'

But my disturbed nights of little sleep are catching up with me, and I fall into a deep and dreamless sleep as Sophie goes on warbling about her secret admirer!

Chapter 8

Sophie

TASH'S DAD AND WENDY have brought us into Ditchfield on a shopping trip. After having hot chocolate at Coffee Heaven – with Alfie sitting in a high chair and crumbling a piece of chocolate cake in his fists –

Tash takes me by the arm and propels me in the direction of Grip, the shop she'd told me about. We are followed at a distance by Tash's dad, Wendy, Alfie and Kezia.

'There he is!' Tash hisses. 'Over there!'

'Who?' I exclaim. 'Oh – you mean the shop assistant you've been telling me about! Yes – I can see why you fell at his feet! He is a total Babe Magnet! NOW I know why you spent so long doing your make-up this morning.' Then I feel ashamed of myself for lusting after another boy. I must be faithful to my Devoted Admirer!

But Tash is no longer looking at the gorgeous shop assistant. She seems to be transfixed by a message which she has just received. 'Oh my God!' she exclaims.

'What's up?' I ask.

'It's . . . it's from Rob! He's dumped Sandi, and he wants us to get back together!'

'Oh – Tash! What are you going to do?'

'I don't know!'

'You could write to Aunty Aggie Advises in *Lurve* magazine,' I suggest, helpfully.

'I think that might take a bit too long. I need an answer NOW. I need to think – help! I can't think!'

Kezia joins us and tells us that Alfie is crying and Wendy wants to take him home – Tash's dad has offered to come back and pick us up later. Tash says she'd rather go home now.

'I want to spend more time with Dad,' Tash explains. 'And I need to think!'

When we get back to Tash's dad's house the phone is ringing. It is Kyle. He explains that he has run out of credit so Mum is letting him use the phone.

'Have you found out who's sending me all that stuff yet?' I ask, urgently.

'Er . . . no. I've only just got up.'

'You're so lazy! Why are you phoning? And why are you talking in such a deep voice? You always do that when you're talking on the phone!'

'Can I help it if my voice is breaking?' Kyle protests.

'But it isn't. Have you been in my room?'

'No! I'm phoning to tell you that Dad's started a snail farm. So I think he's planning to move to France and have an even bigger snail farm. There's more demand for snails over there. They eat them, don't they? I thought I'd better tell you,' he adds.

'A snail farm?' I repeat, slowly.

'Yes – he's feeding them beer to fatten them up. Yesterday, I opened the lid of this snail breeder thing he's got in the garden and there were loads of them in there, drinking beer.'

'Kyle – is this an April Fool? Because it's not April Fool's Day any more.'

'No – it's not a joke.'

'Then you are a moron. What you just described is Dad's slug and snail trap. He gives them beer to kill them, not fatten them up – so they don't eat his plants. Don't you understand? The snails drink the beer, get drunk, fall into the trap and drown.'

'Oh. What a way to go!'

'Do you have anything else to tell me?'

'Er – no.'

'How can anyone who is searching for clues be so clueless?' I exclaim, as I put down the phone. How disappointing! How can I bear this – the Great Unknowing? I can't sleep, I can't eat . . . Is it or isn't it James?

I know I said I couldn't eat, but Tash persuades me to join her for a delicious lunch of spicy chicken wraps, garlic bread and salad, followed by Death by Chocolate. I decide that it would be rude to refuse this as I am a guest in the house so I will have to postpone my Resolution To Give Up Chocolate until I get home. Tash seems distracted. I assume that she is still thinking about the text from Rob, although she won't tell me details – only that she doesn't know what to do!

Tash's dad brings out some old photo albums. Wendy is busy with Alfie and preparations for tomorrow's christening. The photo albums are so fascinating that I almost forget about my secret admirer, and Tash seems equally absorbed.

There are photos of Kezia and Tash as babies, and there are even photos of Tash and me playing together when we were little! And there are photos of Tash's mum . . .

'Does Wendy mind you having these photos of Mum?' Tash asks her dad.

'No – she understands that your mother was a big part of my life,' he replies. He turns to the part of the album which shows photos of baby Tash, and sighs. 'I remember when you were the same age as Alfie is now,' he says gently to her. 'You wore a little pink Babygro, and I'd bounce you on my knee. And now, here you are, all grown-up, attracting the glances of admiring men . . .'

LOOKING AT PHOTOS OF BABY TASH

'Where? WHERE??!' jokes Tash, looking around.

'Everywhere you go.'

'Aaargh! Actually, Sophie's the *real* Total Babe, aren't you, Sofe? She's got a secret admirer . . .'

My stomach lurches because I have just thought of James – I want so him to be my secret admirer!

Dad smiles. 'You *will* both be careful about talking to strangers, won't you?'

'Yes, Dad . . .'

'And steer clear of Internet chat rooms!'

'DAD! We're not a little girls!' Tash exclaims.

'I know – that's why I'm worried. I wish I could put you in a protective bubble and keep you safe forever, but I know I can't. But I'm proud of you – and I love you. Always remember that.'

'Love you too, Dad!' says Tash.

I think about my own relationship with my dad – we don't say 'I love you' very often, but I just *know* that he – and Mum – love me, and I love them. I miss them, and I hope that they will come to their senses about the idea of moving to France . . .

'So what are you going to do about Rob?' I ask Tash. We are sitting on the steps which lead from the living-room French windows down into the small and pretty walled garden. Tash is hugging her knees, her eyes closed, her face tilted towards the afternoon sun. I hope the weather stays as nice as this for the christening tomorrow.

'You've asked me that question about a hundred times, Sofe. And the answer is still the same – I don't know.'

'OK – so maybe Rob isn't the One,' I say. 'But, on the other hand, you'd have someone to go to Lydia's party with – and I hope I'll have someone, too, if Kyle can find out who my secret admirer is.'

'I don't want to get back together with Rob just so I have someone to go to the party with, Sofe! And what if your secret admirer turns out to be Ed?'

'Then I will have to kill myself. Or move to France.'

'Oh, the phone's ringing – Wendy's calling you to take it!'

I scramble to my feet. 'I HOPE that's Kyle with some good news!' I exclaim. 'Wish me luck!'

MOONSTONE

'What's new, Kyle?' I ask, my heart beating fast. All this waiting to find out WHO my Babe of Destiny might be is soooo stressful! In my pocket I have a moonstone – a small, creamy pearl-like stone – which works as an emotional balancer. I feel in need of some emotional balance . . .

'I went to meet Jolene at Froth's today,' Kyle begins, in an extra deep voice (is he deliberately trying to wind me up?).

'Yes – go on . . .'

'We shared a Froth's Soopa Doopa Mocha Rocka.'

'I don't want to know what you drank! Have you found out WHO IT IS?!'

'Keep your hair on! Unless it's on your legs or under your arms or . . .'

'KYLE!'

'OK – I think you'll be pleased. I noticed that James was wearing a wristband just like the one you got sent . . . Oh – and I found out that Mum and Dad definitely *aren't* moving to France. Want to know how I found out? I *asked* them. I didn't want you to go on worrying . . . Sophie? Sophie? Are you there?'

I am dancing round the room . . . I am dancing on air!

'Put the receiver back, would you, Sophie?' Tash's dad asks me. 'You've left it off the hook. Did you have some good news?'

'Oh – yes! *Very* good news!'

'So it *must* be James!' I exclaim, hugging Tash so hard that she gasps for air.

'Delighted.' She doesn't look delighted. She looks confused – and disappointed.

'Cheer up!' I exclaim. 'Rob wants to get back with you – remember? Now we can go to Lydia's party! You and Rob and me and James! Isn't that perfect?'

Tash gives a sickly grin. 'Perfect,' she says, in a flat

voice. 'I'd have thought you'd have been against the idea of me and Rob getting back together. And now you're making out like it's some sort of consolation prize!'

'It's only for Lydia's party – so you won't feel left out! You can dump him again after that, if you like. But at least you'll have given him a chance. Everyone deserves a chance.'

'It hardly seems fair.'

'All's fair in love and war, as they say! Oh – Tash! You don't *really* mind about me and James, do you?'

Tash shrugs – she doesn't look very happy, but she forces a weak smile and says, 'Er, it's fine.' I give her a hug and I really hope she cheers up soon, because nothing can spoil my happiness now – I have found my Babe of Destiny and his name is James! And now we can be together forever because my family is NOT moving to France. I want to HUG Kyle! Tash does look genuinely pleased that I am not moving to France – she gives *me* a hug! I am glad that she has decided not to let a boy come between us – we are still BMF!

Chapter 9

Natasha

SOPHIE IS DRIVING ME MAD. She keeps going on and on about James and the forces of destiny which drew them together, etc. etc. I am beginning to think that my destiny is to murder her.

'Have you forgotten what's happening today, Sofe?' I ask, casually.

'Oh my God! Of course – it's the christening! I'm sorry, Tash – I've been going on about me and James for . . .'

'Forty-five minutes. Since you woke up.'

Time to get ready. Sophie worries that the purple dress isn't suitable for a christening. Then she decides that it isn't suitable for anything and she hates it.

'So why did you buy it?'

'I don't *know*! It's too low-cut at the front and I forgot to bring my padded bra – I've got bigger boobs on my back! I look scrawny!'

'And you think *you've* got problems!' I exclaim. 'This skirt makes my bum look HUGE! Why didn't anyone tell me? Now it's too late – I haven't got anything else!'

'I hate to inform you,' interrupts Kezia, who is wearing a sky-blue Chinese-style silk dress with a pattern of pale flowers and red dragons with flecks of gold, '– but everyone's going to be looking at Alfie, not at you! That's why I decided to wear something simple.'

From her Burberry-check suitcase Kezia produces a wide-brimmed pink hat, which she puts on while looking in the mirror and carefully adjusts it to the right angle. Then she steps into a pair of pink stilettos to match her pink handbag. It is a warm day so she decides to carry her matching pink bolero jacket for now.

'You look amazing, Kez,' I say.

'Thanks! But I *hope* you're not intending to wear those old trainers!' she says.

'What else am I supposed to wear?'

'Tash!' Kezia exclaims. 'You could have brought your school shoes!'

'No way!'

'Is there a problem?' Dad asks, poking his head round the door. 'It's nearly

'YOU LOOK AMAZING, KEZ!'

time to go to the church! You all look lovely, by the way.'

'Dad!' Kezia exclaims. 'Tell Tash she can't wear trainers to the christening!'

Dad looks thoughtful. 'I think the important thing is that you're there – not what you wear,' he says. 'But let me go and have a quick word with Wendy . . .'

He returns with a pair of low-heeled beige sandals with thin cross-straps over the top. They are the sort of shoes I would not normally be seen dead in – but I don't want to be difficult, or hold everyone up.

'Thanks,' I say, putting them on. They are a size too small and my toes protrude over the end. But I decide to rise above the fact I am wearing dreadful shoes for Alfie's sake!

It is a beautiful day. Alfie is a total Baby Magnet, dressed in a white romper suit with a blue jacket and cute blue and white hat. Everyone adores him. I might almost have felt a teensy bit jealous, which is completely stupid – but because of what Dad said yesterday about how he loves me and is proud of me. I just feel happy . . .

Alfie blows very loud raspberries throughout the christening service,

ALFIE

which makes everyone laugh – I am glad that there is something to distract people's attention away from the loud click-clacking noise which my dreadful shoes make on the flagstones in the church.

An hour later and Kezia and I are now officially god-parents! I am very proud of my godson – and I love him . . .

Because it is such a beautiful day Dad and Wendy are able to throw open the French windows and hold the christening party in their garden. It is such a relief to kick off the awful sandals and feel the cool grass between my toes.

'You must be John's daughter!' says a kind-faced, grey-haired lady in a cream-coloured dress and jacket. 'You've got the same green eyes and lovely smile. I'm Wendy's mum!' She is joined by Wendy's dad, a silver-haired man in a brown suit, and they both start discussing how much I look like Dad.

Then Wendy calls Sophie and me into the house and gives us trays of food to pass around. I see that there is a beautiful christening cake with white and blue icing. I'm glad that Mum bought me a camera phone for Christmas – I take a photo of the cake. I have already taken photos outside the church – so I should have plenty of photos to show Mum and Granny. Dad is also taking photos, and so are some of the other guests.

Wendy and Dad unwrap the christening gifts and show them to Alfie. He loves his silver piggy bank, shaking it to make the coin inside rattle. Dad and Wendy, holding Alfie between them, cut the christening cake and everyone raises their glass to Alfie.

'I like champagne!' giggles Sophie – we have been allowed a glass each.

'I think you're meant to sip it, Sofe – not knock it back in one go!'

'Whoops! I was thinking it was water and that I needed to drink three litres of it!'

'Er – no.' My phone bleeps – there is a message from Rob! He wants to know why I haven't replied to the other message he sent me.

'Why haven't you?' Sophie demands, swaying slightly – I think the champagne has gone to her head.

'I don't know!' I reply in exasperation. I am saved from having to answer any further questions by Dad, who calls me over to be in a photo with himself, Kezia and Alfie – Wendy is holding the polaroid camera. Hurriedly I put my phone down on the table where the cake is and join them.

When I get back Sophie is holding my phone.

'I sent a message to Rob for you,' she says.

'You did WHAT?' I gasp, horrified. She had no right to do this! 'What did you say?'

'Er . . . I said you like his . . . his . . .'

'His WHAT?' I ask in an anguished voice.

'Bum.'

'SOPHIE!'

'Please don't be angry! I'm sorry – OK? It was the champagne – I'm feeling a bit strange . . .'

'You'll be feeling even stranger by the time I've finished with you!' I shout. Sophie shrieks as I chase her round the garden . . .

Because it is a special day I have avoided murdering Sophie – but it was a close thing! She has apologised for using my phone and embarrassing me and making the prospect of coming face to face with Rob into something which I shudder to think about . . .

Yes – I *do* like his bum. But I would rather that he did not *know* that I like his bum. As I am still undecided about whether I want to get back together with him, it makes the situation more complicated as he will now think that I *do* – and it will be very difficult to explain to him that I like his bum but not the rest of him, if I decide that I *don't* want to go out with him. I feel like texting him to say that the previous text was from Sophie and that he should ignore it because she's mad – but I am too embarrassed! I want to be an ostrich and bury my head in the sand and pretend that what just happened did NOT happen . . .

* * *

The guests have all gone home, and Alfie has gone to bed. It has been a wonderful day – apart from the 'bum' incident. I have decided to forgive Sophie. She *is* my BMF after all, so we won't let a bum come between us – and I know that she is still stressing about the secret admirer situation, to the point where I feel half-annoyed by and half-sorry for her.

I am looking forward to seeing Mum and telling her about the christening. Sophie is looking forward to seeing James, as she has managed to convince herself that he IS the secret admirer – although she has fleeting but intense moments of doubt. I am trying to be patient and not to be jealous . . .

We drink a litre of water each and say goodnight to everyone – Dad and I give each other a big hug – and then we have relaxing baths and go to bed, having applied face cream, spot cream, all-over body butter and strawberry-flavoured 'lip enricher' – Kezia even lets us use some of her pomegranate stuff and 'Milk 'n' Honey' hand cream. I'm not sure if all of this intensive treatment is going to turn me into a Total Babe – I feel more like some kind of fruit-based dessert!

Chapter 10
Sophie

TASH IS DRIVING ME MAD! She has been obsessing all morning about what Rob must think of her as a result of the 'bum' message. I try to explain to her that boys don't dwell on things like *she* does, and that Rob has probably forgotten all about it by now – but she isn't convinced.

I have happier things to occupy my mind. I am trying to blot out my remaining doubts and concentrate on the fact that I will soon be united at last with my Babe of Destiny. In my mind's eye I see myself and James running towards each other in slow-motion, our arms spread wide – there is a power ballad playing in the background and the music swells as we . . .

'Everyone ready to go?' asks Tash's dad. He has been outside with Kezia, checking that the car is in a fit condition for the journey home. 'I want you to drive very carefully,' he says to Kezia, giving her a hug.

'I will, Dad.'

He hugs Tash. Everyone hugs everyone else and we all kiss Alfie.

I give Tash a special BMF hug – I know she finds it difficult saying goodbye to her dad . . .

'Come again soon!' call Tash's dad and Wendy as we drive away. 'And you, Sophie! Text us as soon as you get back to say you're home safely!'

The first thing I do when I get home is to kiss Kyle.

'Yeuk!' he exclaims, brushing his cheek with his hand. 'What was that for?'

'I said I'd kiss you if my secret admirer turned out to be James. And I'm *sure* it must be! AND it's for finding out that we're not moving to France! In fact, you can have another kiss for that!'

'I'd rather have your sound system!' Kyle replies.

'Help yourself! Just make sure you put it back when you've finished. What's up? You don't look too happy.'

SHE HASN'T REPLIED TO MY TEXT . . .

'Jolene hasn't replied to the last text I sent.'

'When did you send it?'

'Half an hour ago. I'm worried she's dumped me.'

'Why should she? What did you say to her?'

KYLE AND HIS MOBILE

'I said "hello". I keep worrying that I'm saying or doing the wrong thing!' Kyle looks deeply anxious.

'I think you need to chill,' I say. 'Relax – and be yourself. The most important thing is to be yourself. Or, if you can manage it, remember all the advice we gave you and be a Total Babe Magnet!'

Kyle looks confused. 'I don't think I can remember it all,' he says.

'Oh, don't worry! Forget being a Babe Magnet and just be your normal, really great self.' I pat him on the shoulder to show that I fully understand and empathise with the way he is feeling – I know how he feels because I have been there – I know the pain of rejection! I have learned a lot from what I went through when Luke two-timed me, and it feels good to be able to give Kyle the benefit of my big sisterly wisdom experience. I wonder if I should hug him – but think he is still recovering from the kiss. He looks so worried that I decide now is not the time to interrogate him about whether he has been in my room recently.

'You need to learn to trust Jolene,' I continue. 'Trust is so important. By the way, you *haven't* been in my room, have you?'

'Er – no!'

'Right – so you need to trust Jolene. You'll put her off if you keep worrying and being suspicious.'

Kyle looks thoughtful. 'You're right,' he says. 'Thanks for helping me see things more clearly. I think I'm slowly understanding girls and their feelings . . . and I'd really like to find out more. So – if there's anything I can do for you in return . . .!

'Er – don't worry about it, Kyle! And I'm sure Jolene *will* text you. And if she doesn't, then maybe she isn't the one for you. I believe that there is someone out there for everyone, and sooner or later you'll meet the right person. Just like I have with James.'

'Wow,' says Kyle. 'You're better than Aunty Aggie Advises.'

I give Dad a big hug – Mum is at work at the library.

'Dad – I am sooo glad we're not going to France!'

Dad smiles. 'I realised you weren't that keen – but you don't need to worry any more, Sophie – I've been offered a really good job at a school in this country, so we'll definitely be staying!'

'That's great, Dad! I love you!'

Dad looks taken aback – and pleased.

'I love you too, Sophie!' he says. 'And you *will* tell me, won't you, if strange boys are bothering you?'

'Er . . . yes, Dad.' Oh, great – I can so do without parental involvement in my love life, especially when I'm already nervous enough . . .

* * *

'Oh – where *is* Tash?' I ask no one in particular, impatiently twiddling a strand of hair which has fallen across my face. I check my make-up in the mirror for the hundredth time. Why is Tash taking so long? She went home to unpack and see her mum, and promised me that she would come straight round so that we can catch a bus into Bodmington and go to Froth's to see James. Kyle is coming, too – he is hoping to meet up with Jolene. He is being so nice – he even gives me a hug and tells me not to be nervous! How does he know that I'm nervous – is it that obvious? I almost wish he would revert to being a normal brother – help! I have been too successful in transforming him! Or is he being nice because he wants something in return?

Having to wait is making me even more nervous – my stomach is beginning to churn. I fiddle with the blue band on my wrist – the fact that I am wearing it will show James that I am his soul mate and want to be with him. But what if I'm wrong, and it *isn't* him?

At last! Tash is here! We run to catch the bus . . .

My stomach has now gone into the spin cycle. We are entering Froth's . . .

'Tash! What if I'm wrong? It *might* not be him!'

'Sofe – stop stressing and start smiling! Or you'll put him off! And if it's not him, don't worry – it's not the end of the world!'

'Thanks, Tash – you're the best mate anyone could have! I know you like James, too – so this must be hard.'

'It's OK.' She smiles, and squeezes my arm. Tash is really unselfish – I'm so lucky to have her as my BMF!

We find a table near the window. Kyle has his eyes trained on the crowd outside – he has texted Jolene to tell her where we are and to ask her to let him know if she wants to meet up. He has not had a reply.

'Tash! There he is!' I squeak. I have serious butterflies.

James walks over to a nearby table to clear it. He is wearing his blue wristband! It is now or never . . .

'Hi, James!' I call out to him. He looks in our direction.

'Hi!' he says.

This is amazing. I have made first contact with my Babe of Destiny – I think. Encouraged, I get up and walk over to him.

'I love your wristband!' I say. 'Look – I'm wearing one, too!' I give him a knowing smile. My heart is thumping . . .

'Yes – everyone's wearing them! I think it's great that so many people are buying them! Thirst Aid is so important, isn't it? Providing fresh, clean water for everyone in the world has to be the single most important thing!' says James.

My knowing smile fades slightly.

'Er . . . so – have you been giving these wristbands to people?' I ask, in a shaky voice.

'Er . . . no. Why would I do that?' James looks as confused as I feel.

'Um . . . well – it's nice to have . . . er . . . said hello,' I falter. 'Now I'd better . . . er . . . say goodbye! Goodbye! See you in French!'

Feeling incredibly hot, I return to our table. I am aware that my face is the colour of a red hot chilli pepper. I am struggling not to burst into tears.

'Can we leave now, please?' I say, in a very small voice.

But my torment is not yet over. James comes to our table to wipe it. He seems totally unaware of my distress. He smiles at Tash.

'Hi!' he says.

'Er . . . hi!' says Tash, nervously.

James produces a small stubby pencil from his pocket and scribbles something on the corner of a paper napkin. He tears it off and gives it to Tash.

'Call me,' he says. 'Perhaps we could meet up sometime.' He smiles at her, then wanders off.

Tash sits staring at the fragment of napkin in her hand. She doesn't move, or look at me. I think she's in shock.

I remember how unselfish she was when we arrived at Froth's a short while ago – she gave me her full support, no matter how difficult it was for her. Taking a deep breath, I say: 'Go for it, Tash! I think you've just met your Babe of Destiny!'

Tash and Kyle and I are back at home, sitting in my room, listening to *Forgotten Girl*. We are all very quiet. Tash has a dreamy, faraway look on her face – I *know* who she's thinking of, and I am making a determined effort NOT to mind and to go on being unselfish! This

is difficult as I feel like crying with embarrassment and disappointment. In fact, when Tash squeezed my arm on the bus coming home, I *did* cry – briefly. She said she wouldn't contact James if it was going to upset me – but I told her to take no notice of me, and then I smiled my bravest smile. We all have our crosses to bear . . .

I feel sorry for Kyle, who is staring forlornly at his phone. 'She *still* hasn't texted me,' he says, in a flat voice.

'Don't worry, Kyle,' I say. 'If it's meant to be, she *will* text you. And if she doesn't . . . well . . . it's *her* loss. Any girl should be proud to go out with *my* brother!'

Kyle blushes, and grins, despite himself. 'Now you're embarrassing me!' he protests – but he sounds pleased. Twizzler curls round his legs and jumps on to his lap, where he settles down, purring.

'Twizzler's got the right idea,' I remark.

Thinking about others is making me feel better – it makes a refreshing change from my usual 'me me me . . . blah blah blah' stuff – but I still feel bad about making a fool of myself in front of James – and I *do* still like him . . . And WHO is my secret admirer? Mum cornered me when I got home just now, asking questions, wanting to know if I had been meeting up with 'strange' boys! Mum and Dad both seem obsessed with the word 'strange', especially as applied to my love life, and it is making *me* feel strange – I don't feel happy any longer . . .

Tash has drifted off to the bathroom, still in a dream.

'I think Tash is lucky to have a friend like you,' says Kyle, suddenly.

'What?' I ask, surprised.

'I mean – you really like James, right? But you told Tash to go for it and go out with him. That was really unselfish of you.'

'How . . . how do you know all that?' I stammer, wonderingly.

Kyle smiles wanly. 'I may only be your brother,' he

says. 'But I'm not completely stupid!'

'No . . .' I say, slowly. 'No – you're not.'

Tash returns, looking thoughtful. She says that she feels tired and wants to see her mum, who was out when she went home earlier.

I walk downstairs with her. Before we get to the front door, she stops and says to me: 'I meant what I said about not wanting to go out with James if it's going to upset you, Sofe. I'd rather that we stayed BMF – I don't want anyone to come between us.'

'No one ever will, Tash – don't worry.'

'Yes – but I don't want you to feel left out. It doesn't seem right if I have a boyfriend and you don't.'

'It's OK – my secret admirer's still out there!' I say cheerfully, masking the fact that this is now a thought which makes me feel nervous and stressed rather than happy and excited. I don't want to be adored from a distance any longer – I want a normal boyfriend, right beside me.

At that precise moment I stop and stare at the front door – Tash stares, too. Someone is pushing something through the letterbox – it is a folded piece of lined paper decorated with hearts and kisses . . . I feel sick.

'Tash!' I hiss. 'Open the door! Please! I can't stand this any longer – I want to know who it is. Open the door!'

Giving me a brief but understanding smile, Tash opens the door. A boy is on the doorstep, still bending down to push the piece of paper through the letterbox. He straightens up, brushing his hair out of his eyes. He looks familiar – and yet . . .

'Ed?' I say, uncertainly.

'Hello, Sophie.'

'You . . . you look different.'

Ed grins shyly – he actually has a nice smile. Since the last day of term, which was when I last set eyes on him, some sort of extraordinary transformation has taken place. The bushy hair has gone, and has been replaced by a short, casually messed-up style. He is wearing a white, long-sleeved T-shirt and jeans – and a blue stripy wristband. Instead of his usual heavy black-framed glasses he is wearing steel-framed ones in a trendy shape. But it is not his glasses that I notice most – I see through them to the kindest, gentlest, twinkliest brown eyes that I have ever seen. He has a big, warm,

TRANSFORMATION OF ED

BEFORE   AFTER

O.K. – SO HE MAY NEVER BE SUPER HUNK. BUT I HAVE REALISED THAT'S NOT WHAT MATTERS MOST...

generous smile and the lips, which in my ignorance I dismissed as flobbery, are in fact full and sensuous.

'What . . . why . . .?' I stammer. 'Ed – I need to know what's going on.'

'Er . . .? I told my sister that I really liked you,' Ed begins, shyly. 'And she decided to give me a makeover and make me . . . er . . . cool! I'm not sure if she succeeded!' He sucks in his lips nervously – this does look *slightly* like a dog's bottom – but in a funny rather than an off-putting way.

'Yes – I think she did,' I say. 'But – Ed – why did you send me poems and things? Why didn't you just tell me how you felt?'

'I was shy. I'm sorry – I didn't mean to worry you. My sister kept telling me I ought to come and talk to you, but I was worried that you'd reject me. That's when she gave me . . . er . . . the makeover . . . to . . . to . . . give me . . . er . . . um . . . confidence. So you don't mind?'

'No – no, it's cool. Thanks for the chocolates, by the way – they're my favourites!'

Ed smiles his warm friendly smile again – how could I have misjudged him so badly? I feel guilty for not seeing past his previous appearance to the real person inside.

Tash is standing beside me, fascinated.

'What were you posting to me just now?' I ask, looking at the neatly-folded square of lined paper stuck in the letterbox.

'It's a short note just to tell you that it was me who

was sending you things,' Ed replies. 'I thought it was time I owned up. And I wondered if . . . if you'd come to Lydia's party with me on Tuesday? She seems to have invited nearly the whole of Year Ten – it would be great if we could go together!'

'Yes,' I say. 'I'd love to!' Even if he isn't exactly the greatest romantic hero of all time, I feel a huge sense of relief that he is so nice and normal and not creepy like I thought he was! I am more than happy to swap total adoration for total normality!

Ed smiles his warm, friendly smile and gives me his mobile number. I give him mine.

'You and James – and me and Ed,' I say later when Ed has gone home. He came in for a while and said hello to Kyle, who is much happier now as he has had a message from Jolene to say that she had temporarily lost her phone, which is the only reason why she hadn't replied to his messages. Tash seemed to forget that she had been about to go home – she was too fascinated by Ed and his incredible transformation from Official Year Ten Nerd to Official Year Ten Babe Magnet!

'It's quite strange,' I say. 'But I felt so relaxed just now chatting to Ed – in a way I never felt relaxed when I was with Luke.'

'I certainly never felt relaxed when I was with Rob,' says Tash. 'Have you noticed – he's gone very quiet since you sent that "bum" message?'

'That's probably just as well – now that you're with James. Have you texted him yet?'

'No – but I'm going to! I haven't decided what to say! But I feel so much better about going out with him now that I know that *you've* got someone as well! Although . . .'

'What?'

'I don't want everything that's going on with James and me and you and Ed to change things – I still want us to make time to do BMF stuff on our own together, just like we always have. You know I'm not good with too much change!'

I smile at her. 'Don't worry!' I say. 'I feel exactly the same. I *need* BMF time – there is *nothing* more important than that!'

Tash looks relieved. 'That's good,' she says. 'Because other things in my life keep changing – sometimes for the better, of course! But . . .'

'But what?' I ask, gently.

'I *still* feel strange about Barry being with Mum – It's different with Dad and Wendy and Alfie because it's not all happening right under my nose – but Barry's *always* at our house. What if he's moved in while I was away? What if Mum and he get married? What if they have . . . a baby? What if . . . ?'

'Hang on, Tash! What if none of that happens? What if Barry dumps your mum, or vice versa – and you're left to pick up the pieces of her broken heart? You said that you wanted her to be happy – and she is. Wouldn't it be best if Barry stayed? He might turn out to be the best stepdad ever.'

'And cook us delicious spaghetti bolognese every night!' says Tash, musing this over.

'Exactly!' I say. 'And didn't you say that your dad met him once and liked him?'

'Yes – that *does* make me feel better about the whole thing, I suppose . . .'

'So – what are you waiting for? You'd better go and see if your mum's back and find out what your future holds!'

'Thanks, Sofe! You're the best! I'll text you later and let you know how things are going.'

'Yes – and make sure you text James! I want to know what you say to him!'

Tash has gone – and she looked happy, walking tall and strutting her stuff like the Total Babe she is. I obviously have a gift for motivational speaking.

I celebrate the fact that Tash and I are now officially Total Babes Forever with boyfriends by drinking one litre of water and eating a banana. I no longer mind that James fancied Tash instead of me – at least I don't mind *too* much – because Tash's happiness is more important to me. I suppose this makes me a nice person – it makes a change from yelling at Kyle for leaving his smelly socks in the bathroom and all the other irritating things that brothers do, and slouching around in a foul mood when Mum nags me to do my homework.

And now there's Ed. I still can't get used to the idea that he's turned into a Babe Magnet – I expect that the next time I see him his hair will have bushed out, the black-framed glasses will be back, and he will be wielding a toy lightsaber! This is a worrying thought. But his sister certainly did a good job transforming him – and I now know that there is more to him than meets the eye. I feel guilty for having been so superficial and for judging him in the past by his appearance.

I realise that I tried to do the same thing with Kyle, trying to change him into a Babe Magnet! But Jolene seems to like him the way he is, although I think the small improvements in personal grooming, not to mention personal hygiene, probably helped. Ed and Kyle are both nice guys – a little restyling has helped people see it. It's a bit like grooming Twizzler so that you can see what a nice cat he is!

I can't wait to see Ed again. I send him a text suggesting that we meet at Froth's tomorrow – I'm sure Tash will want to go there! Ed texts back to say yes and that he is looking forward to seeing me. I store the message

There is a small chocolate chicken in my room, left over from Easter. It seems a shame to waste it . . . my Resolution To Give Up Chocolate starts from tomorrow!

Chapter 11

Natasha

I AM WALKING ON AIR! Every time I think about James I get a whirly feeling inside – I must see him soon! And I must decide what I'm going to text to him – or he'll begin to think that I'm not interested! I tap a brief message into my phone: HI JAMES! and press send. At least he'll know I'm still alive – perhaps I can think of something more inspired later.

Sophie and Dad have both helped to make me feel better about the Barry situation. But as I walk home I can't help feeling upset that Mum wasn't at home when I got back earlier. She knew I was coming back. I expect she was out having a good time with Barry – he was talking recently about taking some time off work . . .

When I get home Mum and Barry are standing together in the kitchen, grinning as if they have some exciting news to tell me. Oh no! They really *are* getting married – or they're having a baby! I feel my new-found confidence ebbing away . . . I wish Sophie was with me.

'Don't look so worried, darling!' Mum says, giving me a hug. 'It's lovely to have you back – I missed you! You must tell me all about the christening. But first – follow me – Barry and I have got something to show you!'

What is it? Don't tell me – they've already had a baby! And I didn't even realise Mum was pregnant! Or is it an engagement ring so enormous that they have to store it in a separate room?

Mum opens the door to my beautiful blue bedroom. 'Look!' she says. 'Barry and I went shopping this after-noon and look what we found. I think it's the finishing touch to redecorating your room.' My jaw drops. In my room there is a television! 'Oh, Mum! Thank you!' I throw my arms around her. 'You're the best!'

'It was Barry's idea,' Mum explains. 'He convinced me that it wasn't fair that the only person without a televi-sion in their room was you. He's made sure it's working – he even helped to pay for it, which was very kind.'

'Thank you, Barry!' I say, gazing at him in awe. He has just scored several trillion points on the Cool Potential Stepdad Scale. I can't quite bring myself to hug him – but maybe that will come later.

'And he's made spaghetti bolognese for supper!'

How much better can it get?

'And he said he'd do the washing-up so that you and

I can sit down together and have a quiet chat!'

This is too much . . .

After supper I sit down with Mum and show her the photos of the christening. She is very interested in the photos of Alfie. 'He looks a little bit like you did as a baby,' she comments. 'It makes me feel quite broody!' she adds, worryingly.

Mum explains after I make a tactful inquiry that Barry won't be moving in with us – yet. Both she and Barry feel that we all need time to get to know each other and to get used to the idea first. Mum asks me if I think that I can cope with the idea of Barry living with us.

I nod – and then I tell her that I love her.

She says that she loves me, too.

I text Sophie and invite her to come and watch TV in my room! She comes straight round . . .

'You were right, Sofe!' I say. 'Barry is displaying symptoms of being cool.'

We decide that our Resolution To Give Up Chocolate can start from tomorrow, and that we need some chocolate and one or two other snacks to eat while we get down to some serious TV watching in my room. Quality BMF time!

We collect up some coins and walk round to the Minimart. Sophie nudges me. 'Don't look now,' she

QUALITY BMF TIME

says, 'but here come Rob, Luke and Darren!' Darren is in the year above us. Sophie used to fancy him ages ago – but he turned out to be a no-brain bully who liked to call us rude names.

My stomach lurches. I have not seen Rob or heard from him since the 'bum' incident. I feel very hot – this is *so* embarrassing! What if he still wants us to get back together? How do I explain about James? I haven't been in this sort of situation before – with *two* boys wanting to go out with me! Is this what it's like to be a Total Babe?!

There is a burst of over-loud laughter as the boys approach.

'Want to fondle *my* bum, Tash?' yells Darren, coarsely. A little old lady pulling along a shopping trolley looks around disapprovingly.

'Do you like *my* bum?' shouts Luke. 'It IS rather nice, don't you think?' And he turns his backside towards us and wiggles it.

Rob says nothing. He just grins, awkwardly, and avoids meeting my eyes.

'What's going on?' says a familiar voice. It's Kyle, just coming out of the Minimart with a bag of shopping for Sophie's mum.

But I don't feel like hanging around to explain. I have a knotted stomach and my heart has shrivelled to the size of a piece of old chewing-gum. Horrified, I turn and run all the way back to the safety of my room, hot tears streaming down my cheeks. Fortunately, Mum and Barry don't see me, but Kezia and Geoffrey are just coming out of their room and want to know what's going on.

Kezia is sitting beside me on the bed with her arm around me, comforting me, and Geoffrey has gone to fetch me some water, when Sophie arrives, slightly out of breath.

'Rob must have shown that message to all his mates!' I sob. 'They'll ALL be laughing at me! James will find out – I can't go to Lydia's party – my life is OVER!'

I break down in renewed sobs.

'I feel awful!' says Sophie. 'This is all my fault – if I hadn't sent that stupid message . . .'

'It's not your fault that Rob and his mates are stupid, immature no-brains!' I gulp.

'I don't know what I ever saw in Luke!' Sophie says. 'It was bad enough when he was mean to me – but being mean to my Best Mate is worse!'

'They do sound stupid and immature!' says Kezia. 'I hope someone teaches them a lesson!'

'Kyle went after them,' says Sophie. 'I told him what was going on – and he said he'd go and sort them out.'

I stare at Sophie. 'How?' I ask.

Sophie shrugs. 'Don't ask me! Perhaps he's going to have a go at them about the way they've been behaving.'

This is a side of Kyle that none of us is familiar with. Stunned into silence we sit in a row on the bed and watch an episode of a soap called *Desperate Lives*, punctuated by my occasional sobs and sniffs. Sophie passes me a box of tissues and asks if she should fetch me a loo roll from the bathroom. She presses a calming stone into the palm of one of my hands. It feels nice . . .

An hour later, Kyle walks into the room. I am relieved to see that there are no obvious cuts or bruises on him.

'I don't think you'll be having any more trouble from those losers!' he says, cheerfully, wiping his hands on the side of his jeans.

'What did you DO?' asks Sophie, deeply concerned. 'Kyle! What happened?'

'I sorted them out. People like that are cowards. I used to admire Luke Norris – not any more. But I'd say he's developed a healthy respect for *me* because I stood up to him and told him to stop behaving like such a loser where my sister's concerned.'

'Wow, Kyle!'

'OK, it probably didn't hurt that they know that I hang out with a black belt, although Will would never hurt anyone – he only uses karate for self-defence – and he would *never* use his boxing outside of the ring. But people respect him because he's a good guy. Oh, and I made Rob delete that stupid message!'

Sophie stares at her brother. 'Thanks, Kyle . . .' she says. 'But I didn't know you and Will were mates. Doesn't he think we're all nutters?'

'Not any more! And he is my mate! I met him in the park the other day, while you were away, and we got talking. I explained about the mix-up when he was delivering the flyer, and he thought it was really funny. Then I asked him about boxing, because I'm thinking of asking Mum and Dad if I can join the boxing club, and he told me all sorts of stuff about it and karate and other things – and he told me to ask him if I ever needed any sort of help! He was really nice.'

Kezia clears her throat. 'I think you should both be thanking Kyle for standing up for you like that!' she says. 'I hope Alfie grows up to be such a wonderful brother.'

Kyle blushes.

'Thanks, Kyle!' I say. 'I agree with what Kez just said.'

Smiling, Sophie says: 'Well, I'm sorry but you can't have him. He's MY brother, and he's not for sale!'

Kyle grins shyly.

'But seriously, Kyle,' Sophie continues. 'You've been so nice recently – what's got into you?'

'I'm a nice person,' Kyle replies. 'And . . . er . . .'

'Yes? Out with it!' Sophie exclaims.

'I wanted to make it up to you,' says Kyle.

'Make it up to me?' Sophie echoes. 'Make up for what?'

'Er . . . for . . . please don't be cross! I read your diary! I just wanted to find out how a girl's mind works so that I could understand Jolene. I'm sorry – I've felt bad ever since I read it because it was full of personal stuff and . . . well . . . I'm sorry. But I really liked the drawings, by the way – they were brilliant! And you've helped me – I've learned a lot about girls. They're . . . er . . . complicated.'

Sophie goes very quiet. 'Kyle,' she says, eventually.

'Yes?'

'Because you've been so nice, I am not going to kill you – on this occasion.'

'Oh – thanks!' Kyle sounds relieved. 'But – tell me,' he says. 'Do you really wear your knickers inside-out just for fun?'

With a shriek, Sophie chases him out of the room.

Chapter 12

Sophie

I HAVE SQUARE EYES THIS MORNING. Not really – I hope. This is what Mum tells me I'll get if I watch too much television. Last night I stayed at Tash's house and we sat up watching television in her room until her mum came in just after midnight and made her switch it off. Tash complained and said that she wanted to watch round-the-clock rolling news bulletins – but her mum wouldn't let her. I know that what she really wanted to watch were the regular round-the-clock updates from *Celebrity Love Boat* which is sailing round the world. Tash and I are both fascinated by this programme. The best bit is when they evict someone by making them walk the plank! I think there is a lifeboat waiting nearby to pick them up before they get eaten by sharks . . .

'I think it's just as well that we got some beauty sleep last night,' says Tash. 'It's Lydia's party tonight!'

'But I've got huge bags under my eyes!' I complain. 'I may have to give up drinking a litre of water last thing at night – it means I have to get up at least twice to go to the loo! And I think it was a mistake, eating that mango in bed. I'm afraid I've got juice stains on your duvet cover.'

As we get ready for the day I receive a text from Ed. He is looking forward to meeting up with me at Froth's later this morning. My heart does a handspring and my stomach does a twirl!

Tash is busy tweezing her eyebrows.

'I *really* think you could improve on that message you sent to James,' I say, picking up Tash's phone and looking at it. 'I mean, "Hi, James" – it's not the *most* inspired message, is it?'

'Sophie! Put my phone down! Now you've made me tweeze the wrong hair! I look mad!'

'Sorry. But how about saying something like: "Let me put the hot in your chocolate!"'

'Then he really *will* think I'm completely mad!' Tash answers, using an eyeliner pencil to sketch in the missing bit of eyebrow.

'OK – how about: "I'm going to Lydia's party. Want to go with me?"'

Tash looks at me. She is clearly impressed. 'Of course!' she says. 'Why didn't I think of that? Ed's already asked you, so we *could* all go together.'

Tash sends James a message straight away. I can tell she is a bit nervous, but there is no need to worry – James texts back within minutes to say yes.

'YESS!!!' we exclaim, hugging each other.

We all meet up at Froth's. Tash is so nervous at the thought of seeing James that her teeth start chattering – and it is a warm day! I tell her to calm down, even though I am frantically hair-twiddling at the thought of seeing Ed. But as soon as he greets me with a big, friendly smile. I feel myself relax! The talk at our table is mainly about Lydia's party tonight. Lydia herself turns up and swans around, inviting a few more people who had not previously been asked, including Kyle and Jolene.

'It's going to be the BEST party!' she drawls. 'If you're not at my party, you are soooooo not anyone!'

'She is soooo big-headed!' I whisper to Tash. 'I bet she hasn't invited Jasmine!'

Jasmine is Luke's ex-girlfriend, whom he went out with before and after – and probably during – the time that he went out with me. It is a well-known fact that Jasmine and Lydia loathe and detest each other.

SCENE FROM SOPHIE'S SKETCHBOOK :

Hi Luke!

Aren't we soooo beautiful?

LOVELY (NOT) CLOTHES

LYDIA AND JASMINE

'I've heard that Jasmine's planning to gatecrash the party!' says Ed, quietly, so that Lydia doesn't hear. 'With her friend Jocasta. My sister told me. She works at the hairdresser's where they both go – and they were telling her all this stuff.'

'Wow! There'll be fireworks at Lydia's party too, then!' Tash whispers excitedly.

I am opening and closing my mouth like a fish. 'Does your sister work at A Cut Above?' I ask.

'Yes,' Ed replies.

'So the girl who cut my hair was talking about you!' I exclaim.

'Uh oh – what did she say?' Ed grins. 'Her name's Ellie, by the way.'

'She only said nice things!' I reply, smiling. Ed's sister has obviously been working hard on him because he looks even more like a Babe Magnet today, with totally gorgeous, sexy messed-up hair. My stomach does a little flip as I look at him. He says he loves Tash's christening photos – and he wants a photo of me!

Luke is standing nearby. I glance at him. He meets my eye for a tiny fraction of a second, and looks quickly away. Rob is at Froth's as well, sitting with Darren – I don't think either of them has a girlfriend.

Tash looked very uneasy when she first caught sight of Rob, Darren and Luke – but Kyle took a small step towards them and Rob and Darren quickly retreated, and Luke started edging away, looking nervous.

I feel proud – people treat my brother with respect because he's COOL! (My brother is cool – weird.)

Tash is relaxed now, smiling at James as he passes by with trays of used cups. He has been over to say hello

FROTH'S SOOPA DOOPA MOCHA ROCKA

and to tell Tash that he would *really* like to go to the Thirst Aid Concert with her, and he's going to try to get tickets.

We celebrate with Soopa Doopa Mocha Rockas with EXTRA cream and chocolate shavings. We're celebrating the realisation that we can be Total Babes AND enjoy the occasional chocolate moment! There's definitely more to being a babe than following faddy diets and shaving our legs – it's more important how we behave towards other people and each other!

Chapter 13

Natasha

SOPHIE AND I GET READY at my house. We are both really nervous!

'Tash – is this lipstick OK? Or has it smudged all over my face? Do I look like a clown? Do I look scary?'

'SOPHIE! Calm down! Your lipstick's fine. So is the rest of you. I wish I looked as good in a miniskirt as you do. I'm glad you decided not to wear that hat . . .'

Sophie gets another phone call from her mum who seems anxious that Sophie is going to French kiss every boy at the party. She reminds Sophie that her dad will be collecting us no later than eleven p.m. . . .

'Yes, Mum . . .'

Lydia's dad's double garage has been transformed into a fairyland. The entrance to the garage and the trees at the front of the house are festooned with fairy lights and Chinese lanterns. There are outdoor heaters to take the chill out of the evening air. Inside the garage disco lights are flashing and loud dance music is pumping away: Boomph! Boomph! Boomph! Giggling girls are clustered together in little groups, and there is the occasional burst of over-loud laughter from some of the boys, who are hanging around near the long table at the back of the garage where there is a massive spread of plates and bowls of food, and cups of drink.

Ed and Sophie and James and I have arrived together, having met up earlier outside my house so that we could all walk to the party – I was aware of a certain amount of curtain-twitching, and I'm sure that I saw Mum and Kezia's faces peering out at us! I hurried James away – I'm really proud that he's my boyfriend, but I don't think it would be fair to inflict Mum and Kezia on him just yet!

Lydia and Luke sort of lunge towards us – they seem to be joined at the hip.

'Soooooo good of you to come!' Lydia gushes. Who does she think she is – a Hollywood hostess entertaining hundreds of celebrities? In reality she is an annoying girl standing outside her dad's garage wearing my best mate's stupidly immature ex-boyfriend like a new coat! I can feel Sophie stiffen beside me.

Luke looks awkward. I think he would like to get away, but Lydia persists: 'Oh!' she exclaims. 'It's Ed, isn't it?' She gives poor Ed a long hard look. 'He's your *boyfriend*, isn't he?' she says, turning to Sophie and baring her teeth in a huge, dazzling false smile.

'Yes!' hisses Sophie. 'He is!'

Lydia gives Sophie an indulgent, pitying look, squeezes her on the arm – Sophie flinches – and melts away into the crowd saying: 'Must go! Soooo many people to look after! Help yourselves to food and drink, everyone! Fetch me a drink, Luke!'

'She's almost as poisonous as Jasmine!' I say, through gritted teeth.

'*More* poisonous!' Sophie remarks, shaking slightly with suppressed anger.

'It's OK,' says Ed. 'She doesn't bother me! I'm just happy being here with you!' he adds, taking Sophie's hand.

There are more and more people from our Year arriving. There are also stilt-walkers, a magician, a bouncy castle, a trampoline and a human statue, painted silver from head to toe, who perches perfectly still on the little low wall around the edge of the mini-fountain.

'I think human statues are really weird!' says Sophie. 'I hate it when they suddenly turn and look at you – it makes me scream!'

'Want to dance?' Ed asks Sophie.

'Yes – sure!' she says.

They wander off, hand in hand, into the garage where there is now such a throng of people that I can't really

ED LOVES TO DANCE . . .

see what's going on. Occasionally I see Ed's arms rising jerkily above the rest of the crowd. I think he has his own unique style of dancing!

James and I wander round the garden. It is now dark and the coloured lights make everything look magical. We watch the juggler and the magician for a while, and then we have a go on the bouncy castle. After that we are out of breath so we sit on a seat beside a flower bed which one or more of the guests have unfortunately trampled on.

'You're shivering,' says James. 'Would you like to wear my top – it's quite warm.'

Gratefully, I accept. James's top smells of him – I never want to take it off! He leans over and kisses me . . .

'AAAAAAAAAAAARGHHHH!!!!'

James and I sit bolt upright, a thousand icy fingers playing up and down my spine.

'Wh . . . what was that?' I stammer.

'I . . . I don't know!' says James. 'It might be a game of Murder in the Dark.'

I AM NEVER GOING TO TAKE JAMES'S TOP OFF !

'Or maybe somebody really got murdered!' I say, shuddering.

We can hear splashing noises and cries of 'Get off!' and 'Get out of here!' and 'Go away!' And other less polite words.

'It's coming from the fountain,' says James. 'Let's go and see.'

It's hard to get near the fountain because a huge crowd has gathered around it. I find Sophie and Ed.

'What happened?' I ask them.

'I didn't see it,' Sophie replies, 'but apparently Jasmine and Jocasta gatecrashed the party, and Jasmine went straight up to Luke and kissed him – in front of Lydia! Lydia went totally mad and tried to push Jasmine away, and they had a sort of fight and pulled each other's hair and everything. Then Jasmine started running and Lydia chased after her, but Jasmine tripped and fell into the fountain, pushing the poor human statue in by mistake – and Lydia, who seems to have gone round the bend, threw herself into the fountain on top of them! I think they're still in there.'

This I have to see.

I force my way to the front of the crowd, most of whom are now laughing and cheering.

Jasmine and Lydia are both in the fountain, pushing and shoving and hitting each other, and pulling each other's straggly wet hair. The human statue is dragging himself out of the fountain but a lot of his silver body paint has come off in the water, the surface of which shines silver in the moonlight.

'How DARE you spoil my party!' Lydia screams at Jasmine.

'How DARE you go off with MY boyfriend, you spoiled brat!' Jasmine shouts back.

Luke is nowhere to be seen. Lydia suddenly droops. Then, still sitting in the water, she throws back her head and howls:

'DADDDYYY!!! There's a horrid girl! She wasn't invited! DADDDYYY!!!' And she bursts into loud angry sobs.

Two large spotlights at the front of the house are suddenly switched on, lighting up the whole garden. The guests start blinking in the bright light. The front door of Lydia's large house opens and a big man comes striding down the steps. This must be Lydia's father.

'What's going on?' he demands. 'What's all the shouting about? Who screamed? I was on the phone – important call – couldn't easily get away – very annoying to have this interruption, especially with your mother being away at the health farm this week. What the . . .?'

He has stopped by the trampled flower bed. 'I don't believe it!' he roars. 'My prize tulips! Ruined! I knew this party was a mistake! Come along now, everyone – party's over! Time to go home! Lydia! What are you doing in the fountain? Get out at once! And you – the other girl – out you get!'

He looks in the direction of the human statue, who is limping slowly and wetly across the lawn, leaving a silver trail like a weird giant slug.

'And for goodness sake! Someone get that poor man a towel!'

* * *

'That was quite a party!' I say.

'Very memorable!' Sophie agrees.

We are back on familiar BMF territory, sitting cross-legged on my bed, watching the latest update of *Celebrity Love Boat*.

Sophie texted her dad from Lydia's house and asked if it was OK if James and Ed walked us home. He said yes as it was not too late. She asked if she could stay the night at my house – this is so that we can have in-depth BMF post-party discussions in front of my new TV! Her dad agreed on condition that he had a quick word with Mum to check that it was OK and to make sure we get home safely. I suppose he is still worried by Sophie's French-kissing outburst!

I feel much more relaxed about Mum and Barry than I did – and the atmosphere at home is happier as a result. It was fun walking home with the boys, although they seemed shy when we got to my house and wouldn't come in. We agreed to meet up again tomorrow at Froth's, and then they left hurriedly, without kissing us. But the memory of that kiss I had with James earlier lingers on – I am going to see how long I can resist telling Sophie – probably not for long! I know she still likes him, and I don't want to sound as though I'm gloating about the fact that James is my boyfriend! I don't think I need to worry about this as Sophie seems to really like Ed.

'Did you enjoy the party? You and James disappeared for a while,' Sophie remarks.

OK. I'm going to *have* to tell her! 'He kissed me.' My lips quiver – and now I can't stop smiling!

'TASH! You never said!' exclaims Sophie, giving me a playful hit. 'Oh – you're so lucky!'

'I know!' I am still wearing James's creamy brown top with a black CHILLWEAR logo emblazoned across it – I am going to wear it all night! 'How about you and Ed?' I ask.

'We danced. And then we danced some more. He reeally likes to dance! But then we went for a walk round the garden and he talked about his mum and his sister – there's just the three of them – his dad's dead. And he knows a lot about the stars . . .'

'You mean, like Brad Chesthair and Lavinia Drip?' I ask.

'No, no! The other kind of stars – the ones in the sky. He was pointing them out to me – and he's interested in astrology, too, like I am. He's an Arien – the star sign

ARIES – THE RAM (SCENE FROM SOPHIE'S SKETCHBOOK)

CAPRICORN — THE SEAGOAT (SCENE FROM SOPHIE'S SKETCHBOOK)

Aries is sooo compatible with Gemini!'

'James's star sign is Capricorn. I knew you'd want to know, so I asked him,' I say.

'The goat!' Sophie exclaims. 'Now he's the sort of goat I *don't* mind! It's good news for you, Tash, because you're Sagittarius, and Capricorn is totally compatible with Sagittarius. Relationships between Capricorn and Gemini aren't so good, as I said – so maybe things have worked out for the best,' she adds, with a sigh.

'I think they have,' I agree. 'And you definitely don't have feelings for Luke any more?'

'Only murderous ones!' Sophie replies. 'I thought it was really funny the way he disappeared and left Jasmine and Lydia to it! Ed thought it was funny, too. We laugh at the same things – and he kissed me!'

'Sophie! You never said! Is he a good kisser?'

'The best! How could I ever have said that his lips were flobbery? That was so mean of me! They're full and sensuous, and he is reeeally good at kissing! That's why

I'm not *too* jealous of you and James. OK, so Ed may never be Super Hunk, but I've realised that's not what matters most. There's more to life than being a Total Babe – although Ed's a Babe Magnet as far as I'm concerned – he attracts *me*, and that's all that matters! I just like being with him – I'm even looking forward to doing French at school so that I can sit with him. I'm so glad we've got past all that admiring-from-a-distance business. Being the object of a poet's hopeless longing isn't all it's cracked up to be. I'd rather be with someone who treats me like a normal human being – someone I can talk to. Ed agrees – he says he's much happier talking to me than he ever was writing poems to me.'

'That's great, Sofe. But you know what the best thing is – even better than having a boyfriend?'

'Of course . . .'

'Being BMF!' we chorus. 'Best Mates AND Best Babes Forever!'

THE COMPLETE BEST MATES FOREVER

www.piccadillypress.co.uk

⭐ The latest news on forthcoming books

⭐ Chapter previews

⭐ Author biographies

⭐ Fun quizzes

⭐ Reader reviews

⭐ Competitions and fab prizes

⭐ Book features and cool downloads

⭐ And much, much more . . .

Log on and check it out!

Piccadilly Press